* * * * * * *

Many of the creeks leading into the river had already dried up. The poor winter snowfall in the mountains along with the long hot days of summer had caused the drought to spread over the entire valley. To add to the problems was the fact there had been no substantial amount of rainfall for the past several months.

The usually thick green grass that covered the valley floor was rapidly turning brown and dying from a lack of moisture. The watering holes in the valley were slowly drying up as well.

Many of the cattle were already showing signs of stress. With the cattle in such poor condition, they would not bring a good price at market compounding the rancher's problems. Some of the ranchers in the valley would not last another month if a significant amount of rain did not come soon.

The Willard Ranch was the largest ranch in the Elkhorn Valley and spread out as far as the eye could see. It was located at the end of the valley nearest the foothills.

* * * * * * *

D1613232

Other Large Print Editions by J.E. Terrall

Western Short Stories
  The Old West
  The Frontier
  Untamed Land
  Frontier Justice
  Tales from the Territory

Western Novels

  Conflict in Elkhorn Valley
  The Valley Ranch War

CONFLICT IN ELKHORN VALLEY

by
J.E. Terrall

ISBN: 978-0-9992427-3-6

This is a work of fiction. Names, characters, and incidents are either a product of the author's imagination or are used fictitiously, and any resemblance to actual persons, living or dead, is purely coincidental.

Printed in the United States of America

Large print edition printed by www.createspace.com

Cover: Cover photo taken by author, J.E. Terrall

CONFLICT IN ELKHORN VALLEY

To Keith,
Thanks for your support

CHAPTER ONE

The evening was quiet as the sun began to set over the Willard Ranch in Elkhorn Valley. The shadows were growing long when Sam Willard stepped out of his log ranch house and looked over the land. He leaned against one of the posts on the porch and thought about the weather and what was happening in the valley.

Sam watched the bright yellow sun as it slowly sank behind the purple-gray mountains to the west. He could hear the mournful cry of a lone coyote as evening slowly spread over the land. The only other sounds were those of the light breeze as it rustled the dry, brittle leaves of the cottonwood trees near the ranch house. There was also the occasional whinny from one of the horses in the corral next to the barn.

It might have been a fairly typical evening for mid-August if it weren't for what was happening in Elkhorn Valley. Sam was disturbed by rumors he had been hearing in the small town of Shallow Creek, the only town in the valley. The tempers were growing short and as hot as the long summer days.

There was talk of neighbors hoarding water, and of ranchers damning up creeks and streams on their land in order to preserve what water there was for themselves. There was even talk of neighbors fencing off what little open grazing land was left in the valley.

Sam's thoughts were suddenly disturbed by the sound of boots at the end of the porch. Sam turned and saw his longtime friend and foreman coming toward him.

"Evenin' boss."

"Good evening, Casey."

Sam had hired Casey the very first summer he was in the valley. Casey knew more about cattle than just about anyone. Casey was an old cowhand that had been around for a good many years. His skin was weathered and dry like old shoe leather, but his heart was as big as the country.

Casey had worked on the Willard Ranch for the better part of fifteen years. Sam thought of him as more of a partner than a foreman. He was the one man Sam could count on no matter how tough things got.

"That mare's 'bout to have her foal."

"Good. Do you need some help with her?" Sam asked as he pushed away from the post and turned toward Casey.

Before Casey could answer Sam's question, a bullet slammed into the post Sam had been leaning against and pieces of wood flew everywhere. It was quickly followed by the sharp crack of a rifle shot.

Casey quickly drew his gun and fired a couple of shots in the general direction the shot had come from as he scurried for cover around the corner of the ranch house.

Sam grabbed his gun as he dove off the porch. He scrambled behind the water trough next to the hitching post for cover. With his gun gripped firmly in his hand, he lay quietly as he looked around the end of the trough toward the cottonwood trees along the dried up creek bed east of the barn. He couldn't hear or see anything.

Suddenly, there was another bullet that clipped the edge of the water trough sending splinters of wood flying and splashing water into the air. Sam had seen where the second shot had come from and fired back. It was a long shot at best with a pistol, but he couldn't lie there and do nothing. He had to respond to the attack in the only way he could. A rifle would have been a better weapon, but he didn't have one at the moment.

The second shot made it clear to Sam that it had not been a random shooting. Whoever was shooting at him intended to kill him.

"You okay, boss?" Casey called out.

"Yeah. Did you see where those shots came from?"

"No, but my guess would be from down in them cottonwoods by the creek."

"That's where he is."

It wasn't long before Sam's men came running across the yard toward the ranch house. There were eight or nine of them ranch hands, all armed and all ready for a fight. They were ready to take on anyone who had the nerve to shoot at their boss.

"Anybody hurt?" one of the hands called out as he ran up on the porch of the house. He had a rifle firmly gripped in his hands and his eyes were searching for trouble in the direction Sam and Casey were looking.

"No," Sam replied.

The hands remained quiet as they listened for some clue as to where the attacker might be. The silence was suddenly broken as the sounds of a horse racing across the prairie drifted up from near the creek bed. From the sounds of it, someone was in a very big hurry to get away from there. One of the men fired a shot, but the shooter was too far away.

"Anybody see who it was?" Sam asked as he stood up. He slipped his gun back in his holster then brushed the dirt off his pants. He looked to his men for an answer.

"Yeah, but not a good 'nough one to see who it was," one of the ranch hands replied. "The horse was black or dark brown."

"You want us to go after him," Casey asked as he stepped out from behind the corner of the house.

"No, he's too far away. You'd never catch him. It's over for now," Sam said as he ran his hand through his hair and looked toward where the shots had come from.

"You think he'll be back?"

"I don't think so, Casey, at least not tonight," Sam replied.

Sam wondered who could be angry enough with him that they would shoot at him. He was not naïve. Sam knew the stress of times like these drove men to do things out of frustration and despair.

"Maybe we better start puttin' out a watch, just in case," one of the hands suggested.

"Yeah, that's a good idea," Casey agreed. "It could get down right ugly 'round here if we don't get some rain soon."

Sam tended to listen to his men in order to get an idea of what was going on in their minds. From what they were saying, it was clear that they were concerned about what might happen if the weather didn't change soon. They were also thinking that this shooting might be just the beginning of the trouble.

Sam had to agree with them. He was sure that it was turning out to be a long hot summer. Sam knew that when the shooting starts, common sense tends to go out the window. He was thinking that it could be the beginning of a range war.

Sam had seen what a range war could do. Innocent people ended up getting hurt or killed, lives were turned upside down and families were ripped apart. He knew that no one ever wins a range war.

Range wars were ugly things that seemed to take on a life of their own if they were not stopped before they got out of control. Once a range war started, it was like a prairie wildfire. It doesn't stop until everything in its path is destroyed and it burns itself out.

"Might not be a bad idea to keep watch," Sam agreed. "If someone is willing to take a shot at me, they might be willing to try to burn me out.

"Jess, you and Bill take the first watch. I want one of you over by the barn and corrals, and the other over by the haystacks. We need to protect the feed for the cattle."

"Right, boss," Jess replied, then looked at Bill to see if he was ready.

"Keep a sharp lookout. I don't want anyone getting trigger-happy. Make sure of what you're seeing, and don't shoot unless you're sure of your target. Understand?"

"Yes, sir," Bill replied.

"The rest of you get back to the bunkhouse and get some shut-eye. We have a lot of work to do around here in the morning. This place won't run itself.

"Chuck, you and Jake relieve Jess and Bill in a couple of hours. The rest of you work it out so no one stands more than a two hour watch," Sam said.

"I'll see to it," Casey replied.

Sam watched as all the men but Casey walked back toward the bunkhouse. As soon as they were out of sight, Sam turned and looked toward the trees where the shots had come from.

"That was a pretty long shot from those cottonwoods," Sam said as he studied the distance.

"Yeah," Casey agreed. "It'd take a pretty darn good shooter and a lot of luck to hit anythin' at that distance."

"Casey, it could get pretty hot around here this summer."

"Sure could," Casey agreed with a slight nod of his head.

"I want you to see to it that every man is armed and stays alert at all times."

"Yes, sir."

"Right now, you better get back and check on the mare. She may need some help delivering that foal."

"I'll see to it."

After Casey had left, Sam stepped back up on the porch. He stood there for a little while as he watched Casey walk across the ranch yard toward the barn.

Once Casey disappeared into the barn, he turned his attention to the trees where the shots had come from. He began to think about what it was that had brought things to this point.

The Horseshoe River, a wide yet shallow river, wound down through Elkhorn Valley and out the other end at a nice leisurely pace. It was that river that provided life to the valley. The river had given all the ranchers in the valley an ample supply of water for many years. However, this year was different.

The flow of water in the river had become not much more than a trickle across the drying riverbed. Many of the creeks leading into the river had already dried up. The poor winter snowfall in the mountains along with the long hot days of summer had caused the drought to spread over the entire valley. To add to the problems was the fact there had been no substantial amount of rainfall for the past several months.

The usually thick green grass that covered the valley floor was rapidly turning brown and dying from a lack of moisture. The watering holes in the valley were slowly drying up as well.

Many of the cattle were already showing signs of stress. With the cattle in such poor condition, they would not bring a good price at market compounding the rancher's problems. Some of the ranchers in the valley would not last another month if a significant amount of rain did not come soon.

The Willard Ranch was the largest ranch in the Elkhorn Valley and spread out as far as the eye could see. It was located at the end of the valley nearest the foothills.

Sam had as much to lose as anyone, more if the drought continued. He tried to figure out what he could do to ease the problem, but without rain there was little anyone could do.

Sam began to think about the fact he had no heirs to take over the ranch if he should be killed. Without an heir, the ranch would become open rangeland upon his death. There was no doubt his land would be fought over by some of the local ranchers. He wondered which rancher or ranchers in the valley might want to see the Willard Ranch become open rangeland.

Although he knew any rancher would like to have his ranch, there were two individuals that quickly came to mind. The first was Frank Gregory.

Frank Gregory was a man of small stature who had big ideas. However, he lacked the foresight, the knowledge and most of all the ambition to carry them out. He was an angry man with a lot of frustration and hatred stored up inside him. He was also a mean spirited man.

Like many small-minded men, Frank Gregory had a big mouth. He wasn't afraid to say anything whether it was true or not. He was the type of man who didn't like anyone who had more than he had, which meant he didn't like very many people in the valley. He especially didn't like Sam. Frank made it a point of letting it be known to anyone who would take the time to listen, and even some that wouldn't, that he hated Sam.

The north edge of Frank Gregory's spread bordered along the south edge of the Willard Ranch. Frank's hate for Sam had made being his neighbor difficult, if not almost impossible. Sam had tried to get along with Frank, but Frank would have nothing to do with him.

Frank's granddaughter, Marie, was a petite young woman with eyes that were so dark brown in color they often looked almost black. She had shoulder length dark brown hair and it was always combed perfectly. It framed her pretty, almost child-like, face. Sam could never remember seeing Marie in anything other than the finest of dresses from back east. The dresses looked as if they had been designed to accent her very nice figure.

Marie always had a pleasant smile for Sam. There had been several occasions when it appeared she would like to take a few minutes and talk to Sam, but her grandfather would not allow it. He would hustle her off in his buckboard and go straight back to his ranch.

Sam remembered one Sunday afternoon about two months ago when he rode over to Gregory's ranch to call on Marie. When Frank saw Sam riding up, he met him at the gate. Frank had Sam run off at gunpoint by two of his ranch hands. He made it clear that Sam was not to come around again. He told Sam that if he came around again he would shoot him for trespassing.

When Sam took the time to think about it, he could see that Marie was just flirting with him. He often doubted she had any interest in any kind of a serious or lasting relationship.

Frank was not the only one with problems in the valley. Sam knew others in the valley had problems with too little water and not enough grazing land. He thought about who else might want him out of the way. His thoughts immediately turned to Will Carter.

Will Carter was well under six feet tall, but he was heavyset. He could tip the scales at close to three hundred pounds, but he was not fat. He was mild mannered and polite most of the time. Will could be nice and helpful, even down right friendly. The only exception was when he was drinking which seemed to be most of the time lately. Given a few shots of whiskey, Will Carter could be as mean and nasty a man as they came.

For such a large and heavy man, Will could move quickly and was known to be a scrapper when drinking. His fists were as hard as rocks. He could throw a punch that would do a man in if he connected solid with it.

It was also well-known in the valley that Will could easily be influenced by his friends, especially if he had been drinking. Knowing what Will was like after a few drinks, Sam had to wonder if he might try taking a shot at someone if he was egged on.

Sam went inside and sat down at his desk. He put aside his thoughts for the moment. He had just gotten comfortable when he was disturbed by a knock on the door.

"Who is it?" Sam asked as he slid his hand over the grip of his gun.

"It's me, boss."

"Come in, Casey."

Sam watched as Casey opened the door and stepped inside.

"What is it?"

"We got us a nice healthy filly. She delivered it without any problems. They're both doin' fine," Casey said with a grin.

"Great," Sam replied with a big grin.

"By the way, I went down by them trees 'long the creek bed to have a look 'round. I found tracks from a horse. Whoever it was took those shots at yah had been down in them trees for quite a spell."

"What's makes you think that?"

"Well, there was plenty of tracks 'round them trees and 'long the edge of the creek. I could see where his horse had been tied, too. The horse had been there for quite a spell, I'd guess. He ate all the grass 'round them trees," Casey explained.

"That would certainly indicate that whoever it was had been there for some time," Sam agreed. "It makes me wonder why nobody saw him hanging around."

"My guess would be we wasn't thinkin' anybody was goin' ta be shootin' at us."

"I suppose you're right," Sam said with a grin.

"I even seen where that rattlesnake knelt down to steady his rifle 'gainst one of them lower branches on one of them trees. The way he was set, he was plannin' on killin' yah," Casey said with a stern look on his face.

"Why would anyone want to kill me? It sure wouldn't get them any more water."

"I doubt they was seein' it that way. I'd guess their thinkin' was if you was dead, they could overrun the ranch and take what water they wanted."

"You're probably right about that, but we don't have much water, either."

"They don't know that if they been listenin' to old man Gregory."

"You're probably right."

"One other thin'. I found this in the grass next to the tree where he shot from," Casey said as he held out a metal cartridge casing.

Sam took the casing and looked it over. There was no doubt it had been fired very recently.

"Who do we know that uses a 40-60 caliber rifle?" Sam asked looking at Casey for an answer.

"No one 'round these parts I know of, but that don't mean one of our neighbors ain't got one."

Sam looked at the casing again. He wondered who might have such an odd caliber rifle. He hadn't seen one in years.

"Casey, I think I'll go into town tomorrow and have a talk with the sheriff. I'd like to get this stopped before it turns into a full blown range war."

"You think talkin' to the sheriff will do any good?" Casey asked.

"I doubt it, but I still think that it needs to be done. I have to at least try."

"I'll have the hands keep their eyes open. We'll keep a watch on the ranch 'round the clock."

"A good idea. Have them report anything unusual."

"Right, boss," Casey said as he turned and left the ranch house.

Sam knew what he did next might make the difference between all his neighbors getting along, or having them take sides in a bloody range war. Sam certainly didn't want a range war.

    With nothing more he could do tonight, Sam blew out the oil lamp on his desk and went to his room. After washing up, he laid down on his bed.

    Lying with his hands behind his head, he stared up at the ceiling. He had a lot running through his mind, none of it good. It took him a while before he could settle his mind down enough to go to sleep.

CHAPTER TWO

Morning came early to the Willard Ranch, but morning always came early. There were things that needed to be done; and as usual, Sam was up and about before the sun came over the horizon. The first order of business was to feed the ranch hands a hearty breakfast before they began their long day. The ranch hands ate in a dining hall built off the side of the ranch house. Sam often ate with the men, although he had a private dining room in the house.

After Sam had his breakfast and had given instructions to Casey for the day's work, he left the dining hall and went out onto the porch. He looked up at the sky and shook his head. The sky was clear without a sign of a cloud anywhere. To the west Sam could see a few stars in the still dark sky, and in the east he could see the sky was getting lighter. It was going to be another hot, dry day. It was going to be another day without rain, without any relief from the drought, and one day closer to a range war.

Sam walked across the yard toward the barn. Most of his men were already hard at work. One of his ranch hands was leaning against a tree near the corral with a rifle in his hand. He was keeping watch over the corrals and along the dry creek bed.

There was another ranch hand near the haystacks keeping watch over the open prairie.

"How's it going?" Sam called out to the ranch hand closest to him.

"All's quiet, Mr. Willard," the ranch hand called back as he gave a wave of his hand.

Sam waved back to acknowledge that he had heard the ranch hand. He walked into the barn toward the stall where his favorite horse was stabled. Sam could see the head of his horse watching him as he walked toward the stall.

"Good morning, Midnight," Sam said as he put his hand out and gently rubbed the horse's nose.

The large black stallion nuzzled Sam's hand. The horse's ears stood up and his eyes shone with excitement as if to say "Good morning". The horse knew they were going somewhere. There was nothing Midnight liked better than to run in the cool of the early morning air.

Sam took Midnight's bridle off a peg on the wall next to the stall. He opened the gate and went inside. After slipping the bit into the horse's mouth, he slipped the bridle over the horse's head. After securing the leather bridle on Midnight, he led the horse out into the center of the barn.

The horse stood quietly as Sam tossed a saddle blanket on him and smoothed it out. He then tossed the heavy western saddle over the horse's back and secured the cinch.

As soon as he finished saddling his horse, he took a minute to check on the new filly. He smiled as he looked at the filly lying in the straw while its mother stood close by.

"Nice job," he said to the mare, then returned to Midnight.

He took the reins and walked the horse up to the house. The sun had broken over the horizon by the time Sam tied the horse to the hitching rail out front. He went into the house to retrieve his rifle from above the fireplace. He checked it to make sure it was loaded and ready for use, if needed. Just as he was about to go back outside, he heard someone at the door and turned to see who it was.

"Boss, can I have a word with yah?"

"Sure, Casey. What's on your mind?"

"Yah goin' into town?"

"Yeah. Why?"

"Me and the boys was thinkin' maybe yah shouldn't go into town alone after what happened yesterday. It might be a good idea if yah took a few of the hands with yah, just in case there's trouble," Casey suggested.

"If it means anything to you, I gave that some thought myself. I'm going into town to see the sheriff. Now, if I arrive with a bunch of ranch hands armed to the teeth, what kind of a message do you think that's going to send to the sheriff?"

"Well," Casey said thoughtfully, "I guess it would tell him we ain't goin' to take nothin' off no one. And if he can't do his job, we'll do what we need to do to protect the ranch."

Sam could not help but smile. Casey was always straightforward. There was no beating around the bush for him. It was clear where Casey stood and what he was getting at. He didn't want his boss riding into trouble without having help close by. Sam also knew Casey didn't like the sheriff.

Sam didn't think all that much of the sheriff, either. But this was no time to throw fuel on the sparks of a fire that was just waiting for someone to start it up. Sam would not back down from a fight if it was brought to him, but he was not going to be responsible for starting it.

"I guess that's what it would say, but I think I'll just ride into town and have a nice peaceful visit with the sheriff. I hope it does some good and he does his job."

"But what if it don't do no good and he doesn't do his job? Then what, Boss?" Casey asked.

"Then we do what we have to do to protect the ranch, even if it means fighting."

Casey looked at Sam as he rubbed his chin. It was easy to see Casey didn't completely agree with his boss's assessment of the situation, but he rode for the brand and would do as he was told. He was convinced there was going to be trouble, and he was all for being ready for it. He had also made it clear he didn't like the boss going into town alone. He had said his piece, it was time to shut up and get back to his own business of being the foreman.

Sam saw the look in Casey's eyes. He didn't want Casey to leave without saying something that might ease his concerns.

"Tell you what, Casey," Sam said before Casey had a chance to turn around and head back toward the door. "You get the men ready for trouble and keep an eye on things around here. If I'm not back by sundown, you get a few men together and come find me."

"Yes, sir," Casey replied, then turned and walked out of the house.

Sam watched Casey as he left the ranch house and walked across the yard toward the bunkhouse. He knew that Casey was worried, but now was not the time to add to the problems. If the sheriff didn't do anything to cool down the tempers of the ranchers that were doing the most complaining, then Sam would do whatever it took to protect his ranch and cattle.

Sam picked up the rifle from the table and went outside. He slid the rifle into the saddle scabbard. Sam untied the reins, put his foot in the stirrup and swung up into the saddle.

Once in the saddle, Sam turned his horse and started down the lane to the road that would lead into town. He gently nudged his horse in the flank with his spurs and the horse started off at a trot. It was a nice even trot that would cover ground rather fast, but was not tiring to the horse or rider. It was a gait Midnight liked and Sam didn't mind.

Once they reached the end of the lane, Sam turned the horse toward town. It would have been a nice morning for a ride if it had not been for the trouble brewing in the valley. Sam's mind was occupied with thoughts of what might happen if tempers were not cooled down, and soon.

Sam knew there were only two possible ways to cool tempers. One was to have it rain. It would have to be a heavy enough rain to put some good moisture back in the ground and to put a good amount of water in the watering holes. From the look of the sky this morning, there was very little chance of that happening.

The other way to get people to cool their tempers was for the sheriff to get everyone together and get them talking. When people are busy talking about their problems and trying to work together to find solutions, it's harder for them to fight among themselves. Sam was sure that there were at least two ranchers that weren't interested in trying to find solutions. They were only interested in placing the blame on someone.

Although Sam's mind was occupied, he continued to keep his eyes moving. He searched the countryside looking for any sign of trouble. He didn't want any surprises, nor did he like the idea that someone might be out to get him. He knew there were several places along the road to town that would provide cover if a person had a mind to bushwhack him. He was especially alert in those areas, but he didn't see anyone.

The ride toward town gave Sam a chance to see what condition a few of his neighbor's ranches were in. Some were in about the same condition as his ranch, but some were worse off.

As he rode past Will Carter's ranch, he noticed there were several cows looking raw-boned and weak. It was easy to see they were not getting enough water or feed.

Sam could see cows standing next to a dried up watering hole. Carter's ranch was no different from the others in the valley. Sam was sure there were other watering holes on the ranch that had some water in them. It made him wonder what Carter was doing to make sure his cattle were taken care of. The fact these cattle had no water and there was no one seeing that they were moved to someplace with water concerned him. His first thought was that Carter might have already given up.

On the other side of the road was Phil Walker's place. There were only a few cattle that Sam could see from the road, but they looked to be in better condition than Carter's cattle. It was clear by the look of the land that Walker had his problems like the rest in the valley. It was also clear he had not given up. What Sam had seen on his way into town was disturbing to him.

When he arrived in the town of Shallow Creek, the street was empty except for two men sitting in front of the Red Garter Saloon across the street from the Sheriff's Office. Sam was not sure who the men were, but from the looks of them they were not cowboys. As he got closer, he could see how they wore their guns, low and ready. The first thought that came to Sam's mind was these two men were gunmen for hire.

Sam rode up in front of the Sheriff's Office. He stepped out of the saddle and looked across the street at the men while he tied his horse to the hitching rail. He wondered if they were just passing through or if someone had hired a couple of new ranch hands, more correctly put, a couple of gun hands.

Sam turned and went into the Sheriff's Office. He found Sheriff Becker sitting at his desk with his feet up. Becker made no effort to take his feet off the desk. The look on Becker's face gave Sam the impression he might have been expecting him.

"Mornin' Sheriff," Sam said politely.

"Mornin' Sam," Sheriff Becker replied as he glanced up at Sam. "What brings you all this way to town?"

"I want to report a shooting," Sam said as he sat down in front of the desk.

"Oh. Who'd you shoot?" Becker asked with a hint of a smile on his face.

Just from the way Becker was acting, Sam got the feeling he already knew about the shooting. And if he was right, Becker knew it was Sam that had been shot at.

"I didn't shoot anyone. Someone took a couple of shots at me."

"Oh. Well, it looks like they missed," Becker said with a slight grin showing at the corners of his mouth.

"Yeah. They missed," Sam replied, quickly realizing Becker didn't care.

"What do you expect me to do about it?"

"I expect you to do your job," Sam said with a matter of fact tone in his voice.

"And just what do you think my job is?" Becker said sarcastically.

"To keep the peace and to investigate crimes. To my way of thinking, shooting at someone is still a crime in this territory, at least it was before you became sheriff," Sam said, even though he knew he was not going to get any help from Becker.

"I doubt there would be any tracks I could follow with the ground so hard and dry. But then you've got plenty of water."

"What's that have to do with being shot at?" Sam asked, wondering just what Becker was getting at.

"I've heard tell you've dammed up a couple of the streams that flow through your property so you can force some of your neighbors off their land. To my way of thinkin', that might make your neighbors rather unhappy."

"And where did you get that bit of information?" Sam asked, as he grew increasingly hot under the collar.

"I just heard," Becker said with a grin.

"Well, whoever told you that is a bold-faced liar."

"Maybe," Becker said with an even bigger grin.

There was no doubt in Sam's mind Becker was enjoying the fact that Sam had been shot at and that he was irritating Sam. Sam also got the feeling Becker had taken sides with some of the small ranchers who were jealous of him. If the two or three troublemakers in the valley were able to persuade the others that Sam had dammed up the streams to cut off their water supply, there was no doubt things could get real nasty, and real soon.

"If you want to get off your fat ass, you're more than welcome to come out and see for yourself that I have not dammed up a single creek," Sam said.

"Careful who you're talking to like that," Becker warned, the grin quickly fading from his face.

"I knew it wouldn't do any good to talk to you. For some reason that I don't understand, you seem to want a range war. Well, let me point out one of the realities of range wars for you. If a range war gets started, you just might find yourself one of the casualties," Sam said as he stood up.

"Is that a threat?" Becker asked sharply as he jerked his feet off the desk and stood up.

"No," Sam replied casually now that he had Becker's undivided attention.

"You threatened me," he retorted sharply.

"No. I was just pointing out your position if a range war starts. When a war like that breaks out, it doesn't seem to care who gets hurt or killed. And whether you like it or not, you'll be right in the middle of it," Sam said feeling a little better that Sheriff Becker was at least listening to him now.

With that said, Sam turned and walked out of the Sheriff's Office. He knew he had given Becker something to think about. Whether he would listen to the warning was another matter. Sam sort of doubted it. He knew Becker was not a quick thinker. It took him time to make even simple decisions.

He was also not a man to do anything without some backing from others. Either way, Sam was reasonably sure Becker would start thinking before he stuck his neck out too far.

CHAPTER THREE

As Sam stepped out of Sheriff Becker's office onto the boardwalk, he stopped and looked across the street at the two men sitting in front of the saloon. One of them was tipped back in a chair leaning against the wall of the saloon. He didn't look like he was paying much attention to what was going on around him. The other one was sitting in a chair whittling on a piece of wood. He seemed to be more interested in the wood than in anything else.

Sam started across the street toward the saloon. Although he had no reason to believe these men were here to cause him trouble, he didn't take his eyes off the men as he moved closer. When approaching the two men, one of them glanced up at him, but that was all. He didn't seem to be the slightest bit interested in Sam.

Sam walked past them and into the saloon. He stepped up to the bar and ordered a cup of coffee. He had carefully chosen a place at the bar where he could see the front door clearly in the large mirror behind the bar. The bartender poured a cup of coffee and set it down in front of him.

"How's it going, Sam?"

"Not so good, Jake. If we don't get some rain soon, this whole valley could go up in flames."

"Yeah, I know what you mean. Will Carter was in here the other day drinkin' too much, as usual. He was tellin' anyone who would listen, and some of them that wouldn't, that you've got the creeks and streams dammed up 'cross your place, cutting off the water to the other ranchers."

"Hell, Jake. You know me better than that."

"I know you wouldn't do anything like that. You've done more to help these ranchers get settled in this valley than anyone else. I tried to tell Will that, but he wasn't havin' any part of it. You know how he gets when he's been drinkin'."

"Yeah, I know. The problem is that some of the ranchers in this valley will believe him because it's easier for them to blame me than to blame the weather," Sam said in frustration.

"I guess that's human nature."

"Say, what do you know about the two sitting out in front of your place?"

"Nothin' really. They rode in here yesterday evenin'. They had a couple of beers and then left. This mornin' they showed up out in front again and have been sittin' there ever since."

"Any idea what they're waiting for?"

"Nope."

"Have they asked about anybody?"

"Nope. I'll say this much, they don't look like ranch hands' though. They look more like gunfighters to me."

"I'll have to agree with you on that. If they are gunfighters, there's real trouble brewing," Sam said with a disappointed look on his face.

"You got that right," Jake agreed with a nod of his head.

"Well, there's nothing I can do about it here. I guess I best get back to the ranch," Sam said, then took another swig of coffee.

"You watch your back out there, Sam," Jake warned. "There are some people that might believe what Carter is sayin' about you."

"I will, and thanks," Sam replied then drank down the last of his coffee.

Sam dropped a coin on the bar to pay for the coffee, then turned and walked toward the door. As he stepped out onto the covered boardwalk in front of the saloon, he looked off to the side toward the chairs where the two men had been sitting. They were gone and it caused him to worry. He had been shot at once already, which tended to make him rather nervous and a little on edge. Not knowing who they were, or why they were there caused Sam to reach down and put his hand on his gun.

Sam slowly backed into the saloon doorway as he looked up and down the boardwalk. He hadn't remembered seeing any horses tired out in front of the saloon when he came in, and there were none now. The two men had apparently not expected to leave town soon. If that was the case, they were probably close by, but where?

Sam backed into the saloon as he continued to look up and down the street, closing the swinging doors as he backed up. At this point he had no reason to think he was about to be ambushed, but with what had happened at the ranch yesterday he felt caution was the best course of action.

The first thing he noticed was that the street was empty. There was no one on the street and none of the local merchants were anywhere in sight. There were only two horses tied to the hitching rails along the street. There was his horse across the street in front of the Sheriff's Office, and another in front of Ma Barker's Boarding House just down the street.

It was not like Sam to be in town at this hour of the morning so he really didn't know for sure if this was normal for the middle of the week. Sam knew Shallow Creek was not a hub of activity at this time of year, but it still seemed a little too quiet to suit him. What he did know was the tension in the air was very high. Even the hair on the back of his neck was letting him know that something was not right.

"What's the matter, Sam?" Jake asked as he watched Sam.

"I don't know. The two that were sitting out here when I came in are gone," Sam said without turning around to look at Jake.

Jake came around from behind the bar and walked up next to Sam at the door. He looked up and down the street while still standing inside the saloon.

"I wonder where they went," Jake said.

First they were there and now they were gone. Jake had not seen them leave the porch of the saloon.

"I don't know," Sam said as he continued to look around.

There was a long period of silence between the two men before Jake spoke up.

"What are you going to do, Sam?"

"I don't have much choice. My horse is on the other side of the street."

Jake didn't like the smell of this any more than Sam. Bushwhacking someone was a coward's way of doing things. Jake didn't like cowards.

"Let me get my shotgun. I'll cover you," Jake said, then turned to retrieve his shotgun from behind the bar.

Sam waited at the door and continued to look around. He thought he saw a flash of light down the street a little ways. He wasn't sure what it was, but it caused him to reach down and put his hand on his gun again. The flash of light was like the sun reflecting off of something shiny like a piece of glass or a mirror, or possibly something else like the gun barrel of one of those fancy nickel-plated guns.

Whatever it was, it alerted every nerve in Sam's body.

"Jake, I saw something over there between Ma Barker's and the Sheriff's Office," Sam said as Jake came up behind him.

"Any idea what it might be?"

"Yeah," Sam replied after giving it some thought.

"What do you think it was?"

"I think it was a gun barrel. I noticed that one of the men sitting on your porch had one of those fancy nickel-plated pistols. Wait here and keep an eye open. I'm going around back."

"Sure thing," Jake replied as Sam turned away from the door.

Sam hurried to the backdoor of the saloon. He carefully drew his gun, then slowly opened the door and peered out. There was no one out back.

He stepped out behind the saloon and moved quietly toward the corner of the building. Very carefully, he took a peek around the corner. From the back of the saloon he could see down between the buildings on both sides of the street. He found himself no more than twenty-five feet or so from one of the two men that he had seen in front of the saloon earlier.

The man closest to him was standing at the front corner of the saloon with his back to Sam. He had a gun in his hand and was looking around the corner as if he was watching for someone.

Sam could also see the other man. He was across the street between the buildings, sort of hunkered down behind a rain barrel at the corner of the Sheriff's Office. Sam could see the nickel-plated six-gun in his hand.

It quickly became obvious that they intended to ambush Sam by getting him in a crossfire as he walked across the street to his horse. Sam pulled back and leaned up against the building. He knew he could take the one on his side of the street without any difficulty, but he wasn't so sure if he could get the other one. The one across the street had to be a good forty feet or more away. He also had a little more cover that would make it harder to get a good clean shot at him.

Suddenly, Sam had a thought. These two were ready to bushwhack him right in the middle of town, right next to the Sheriff's Office. Sam had not seen their horses so it was obvious they were not prepared to make a fast getaway.

This caused Sam to think a little more about Sheriff Becker. He had to wonder if Sheriff Becker was a part of the ambush, or if he was sitting in his office waiting for these two men to do their nasty deed?

Sam took a minute to think. He knew Becker was not a gunfighter. Although he was a sheriff, he couldn't handle a gun very well. He never did anything without several deputies to back him up. Sam doubted the sheriff had the backbone to get directly involved in an ambush, but it sure looked as if he wasn't going to do anything to prevent one.

Sam could speculate all he wanted, but there was no proof Sheriff Becker was involved. He also knew the time for speculation was over. It was time for him to make his move. He carefully checked his gun and prepared himself to do battle with two men he didn't even know. Sam had no idea how good they might be with guns. He was leery, but if he was going to get out of this alive he had to do something and do it now.

Sam took in a deep breath, then let out a long sigh. He took a quick peek around the corner to make sure the two bushwhackers were still where he could get to them. Using the corner of the building as cover, he raised his gun and pointed it at the back of the man closest to him.

"Put your hands up and drop the gun," Sam said with a strong tone of authority.

The man froze, then slowly stretched out his hand with the gun in it to the side. He let the gun fall from his hand to the ground.

"Slowly back up. Don't turn around and don't make any sudden moves if you want to live."

The man began backing up, very slowly. As he did, he stayed close to the building. His movement caused Sam to lose sight of the man across the street for just a moment. When he was able to see the rain barrel across the street again, the man was gone. Sam quickly moved up behind the man and pushed his gun into the man's back.

"Where's your friend?" Sam asked as he pushed the barrel of his gun harder into the man's back.

"By the time you find out, you'll be dead," the man said with a tone of defiance in his voice.

Sam needed to act quickly. He knew the only possible help he would get was from Jake, but he had left Jake watching out in front. Becker would be no help, either. He would just as soon see Sam dead anyway.

Sam quickly raised his gun in the air and brought it down hard on the back of the man's head sending him sprawling to the ground. He turned around just in time to see the other man coming around the corner. They saw each other at about the same time. Sam pulled the trigger and the gun jumped in his hand as the sounds of gunfire filled the air. In a matter of a split second several shots had been fired.

One man was lying in the dirt dying of a gunshot wound to his chest. The other stood with blood trickling slowly down his arm. The last thing Sam had wanted to do was to kill anyone, but this one had given him no choice in the matter.

As Sam walked toward the man he had killed, Jake stepped out the backdoor with his shotgun in his hands. Jake looked at the man Sam had killed, then looked at Sam as he walked up to him.

Suddenly, Sam heard something move behind. Jake heard it, too. As Sam swung around, he saw the man he had hit on the head going for a gun tucked in his belt. Jake saw him at the same time and pulled the trigger on his shotgun without a moment's hesitation. The blast of shot ripped through the man before he was able to pull the gun up to take aim at Sam. There were now two men lying dead behind the saloon.

Sam looked at the dead man on the ground, then slowly turned and looked at Jake. There was no doubt in Sam's mind that Jake had saved his life.

"Thanks," was all Sam could manage to say at the moment.

Jake did not reply. He simply nodded his head slightly and turned to look at the man he had shot.

"Who are they?" Sam asked. "And why were they after me?"

"I don't know," Jake replied, then turned back to look at Sam. "You better go over to doc's and get that arm looked after."

Sam looked at his arm. It wasn't bleeding very badly. It was really nothing much more than a scratch, but it was beginning to burn a little.

"You're probably right," Sam replied.

"I'll have these two taken care of," Jake said.

"Thanks. When the sheriff decides to show up, tell him I'm at Doc's getting looked after. He will probably be delighted to know I got shot, but disappointed as hell to know I wasn't killed."

"I'm sure you're right."

Jake watched as Sam turned and went around the corner toward the doctor's office. He waited for what seemed to be an unusually long time for Sheriff Becker to show up. He was convinced the Sheriff was waiting to make sure all the shooting was over before he stuck his head out of the office.

Finally, the Sheriff came out the backdoor of the saloon with his gun in his hand. He looked around and saw the two dead men lying on the ground.

"Did Sam kill them?"

"Not really," Jake said slowly and with a slight grin on his face.

"What the hell's that suppose to mean?" Becker asked angrily.

"I killed that one," Jake said as he pointed to the one killed by the blast of his shotgun. "Sam killed the other. These two tried to bushwhack him. You got any idea why?"

Jake stood looking at Becker's face for some kind of reaction. He really didn't expect an answer.

"How the hell should I know?" Becker asked angrily.

"Just wonderin'," Jake said with a grin.

"Where's Sam know?" Becker asked without asking what had happened.

"At Doc's office. I know it's disappointing for you to know he was only slightly injured."

Jake noticed a rather disgusted look on Sheriff Becker's face. It struck Jake as being a little strange that Becker didn't seem at all interested in what happened, but he knew that Becker didn't like Sam. Jake was sure that Sam had been right. Becker probably was disappointed that the bushwhackers had not killed him.

Becker glared at Jake, but said nothing more. He turned on his heels and walked around the corner of the building. Jake smiled to himself, pleased that Becker had not gotten rid of Sam.

It wasn't long before the smile disappeared. He knew Becker would not give up hope that someone would kill Sam.

CHAPTER FOUR

Doc Miller's office was located above Potter's General Store near the edge of town. Sam went up the stairs along side the general store and walked into Doc Miller's Office. He was holding his hand over the wound on his lower arm in an effort to slow the bleeding. The lower part of the sleeve of his shirt was dark with blood. There was a small amount of blood seeping out from under the cuff of his shirt and running down between his fingers.

Doc Miller was sitting at his desk with his back to the door when Sam came in. He had heard the gunshots, but based on past experience he had found it was better to stay in his office in case someone needed him. In this way he would be easier to find him. He turned around to see who had come in.

"Hi, Sam. What brings you here?" Doc asked, then he noticed the blood on Sam's arm.

"What happened to you?" Doc Miller asked as he stood up.

"A couple of men tried to bushwhack me. They almost succeeded," Sam said as he glanced down at his sleeve.

"Come over here and let's take a look at it. Sit down next to the table."

Doc Miller poured some water from a pitcher into a bowl. He set the bowl on the table, then walked across the room to a cabinet.

"I heard some gunshots. Anyone else hurt?" Doc Miller asked as he returned to the table with a handful of bandages.

"No one you can help, Doc," Sam replied while looking up at him.

Doc Miller stopped and looked at Sam's face. From the expression on his face, there was no doubt what he meant.

"Well, let's see what we have here," Doc Miller said as he sat down beside Sam.

Doc Miller carefully rolled Sam's sleeve up above his elbow and took a good look at the wound on his arm. The wound didn't look too serious. The bullet had not broken any bones or cut any major arteries or veins. It had been a pretty clean shot and didn't look as if it had done any real damage to Sam's lower arm.

While Doc washed out the wound, he asked what happened. Sam explained how the men had tried to bushwhack him and how Jake had saved his life.

Just as Doc Miller was putting the finishing touches on the dressing over Sam's wound, the door to his office flew open with a crash. It startled both Sam and Doc Miller. They turned and looked toward the door and saw Sheriff Becker standing in the doorway. He had a gun in his hand and it was pointed at Sam.

"It's about time you showed up," Sam said as he looked at Becker.

"You're under arrest," Becker snapped while holding his gun on Sam.

"What the hell do you think you're doing?" Doc Miller asked angrily.

"I'm arresting Sam for shooting down two men in the street," Becker said without taking his eyes off Sam.

"You seem to have gotten your facts a little mixed up, Sheriff. First of all, they were shot down in the alley behind the saloon. Secondly, they were trying to kill me. I was just defending myself."

"I don't know that," Becker shot back.

"Like hell you don't. You were probably involved in it."

"I didn't have anything to do with it," Becker insisted, his voice suddenly showing more of a defensive tone.

Sam did not miss the change in Becker's voice. It gave him some indication that what he thought about Becker might very well be true.

"That's just it. You knew those two were going to try to kill me. You didn't have anything to do with it except to let it happen. As far as I'm concerned, that makes you a part of it."

"You can't prove that," Becker retorted.

"I think you knew why those men were in town. I wouldn't be surprised if you know who they were and who paid them to try to kill me," Sam said as he glared at Becker.

"You can't prove that," Becker blurted out again, his courage slowly evaporating like water under the hot sun.

"Maybe not right now, but if I find out you did nothing when you knew those two were out to kill me, I'll come after you and you'll wish you had never been born."

"You can't threaten me like that," Becker insisted, but the slight quiver in his voice gave away the fact that deep down inside he was afraid of Sam.

"You'll never learn, will you? That was not a threat. That was a promise," Sam said angrily.

There was no doubt Becker knew Sam meant what he said. Sam could see the scared look in Becker's eyes and noticed a slight tremor in Becker's hand. He knew Becker didn't have the nerve to do anything by himself. He had to have someone else to back him up, or to do his dirty work for him.

Sam knew Becker wouldn't have come here to arrest him by himself if he had known Sam had only a slight injury to his left arm. The only reason he was here now was because he thought it would be easy to arrest Sam in Doc Miller's office, since he was wounded.

"I'm still arresting you. I can hold you in jail until the circuit judge gets here late next week."

Although Becker tried to sound brave and ready to take Sam off to jail, but there was a tremble in his voice. He had the drop on Sam, but he was still scared of him. He had good reason to be afraid. He knew Sam was a rancher, but it was no secret around the valley that Sam could handle a gun and handle it well. Although he had no first hand knowledge, Becker had heard Sam was as fast as most gunfighters, but more importantly he was very accurate with a handgun.

"You are not taking my patient anywhere," Doc Miller insisted, his voice showing how angry he was with Becker and how little respect he had for him.

"I'm the law, Doc. If I say he's goin' to jail, he's goin' to jail," Becker stated flatly but nervously.

"You don't run this town, Becker. If you take Sam to jail, I'll have the town council run you out of town on a rail. You may be the county Sheriff, but you only have authority within the town limits because the town council said you could. They can take that authority away from you just as fast and just as easy as it was given to you. Maybe it's time for this town to hire its own town marshal. One that doesn't play favorites, and one who uses at least a little common sense."

"Well, until the town gets its own lawman, I'm the law here. I'm still taking him to jail," Becker insisted.

"Sam isn't going anywhere. He will be around when the judge gets here to have a hearing," Doc Miller said with a tone of authority in his voice.

Becker looked from Sam to Doc, then back to Sam. He didn't know what he should do. He knew that Doc had a lot of pull in the town and could get the town council to revoke his authority.

For the first time he started to think about what he was doing. He began to think he might have bitten off more than he could chew. He also began to think about what might happen if he did arrest Sam.

If he tossed Sam in jail without the full support of the town council, he would loose what little credibility he had with the town folks. He might also lose the support of some of the folks that don't live in town. Becker already knew some of the town folks didn't think much of him. There had been talk by the town council about hiring a town marshal for some time. Up until now they had done nothing about it, but arresting Sam Willard could very well change their minds. Sam was well liked by most of the town's businessmen. He had done a lot to help them get established in Shallow Creek.

Another thing he hadn't thought about but was beginning to slowly seep into his brain was what else might happen if he locked Sam up. There was a very strong probability that Sam's men would come into town and get him out of jail, one way or the other. They might even burn the jail to the ground and kill him in the process. There was no question Sam's ranch hands were fiercely loyal to Sam, and Becker knew it all too well.

The more Becker thought about it, the more he was convinced Sam's men would come and get their boss out of jail. He was also positive they would kill him while doing it. Becker knew he would not be able to get enough deputies together to stop them.

Becker had to do something to save face in front of Doc Miller, and he had to do it before this went any further. He slowly began to realize Doc Miller had given him a way to get out of this without looking any more like a fool than he already did.

"Well, if you'll see to it Sam shows up for the hearing, I'll let him go," Becker finally conceded.

"I'll make sure he's there."

"But I'll hold you responsible if he doesn't show up for trial."

"Fine. Now put that damn gun away before you hurt yourself with it," Doc said in disgust.

Becker looked at Doc, then back at Sam. Doc's comment angered him. He hesitated for a second thinking he might change his mind and lock Sam up anyway, but logic and good sense managed to prevail in spite of his anger.

Becker reluctantly put his gun back in his holster. After looking from Doc Miller to Sam, he turned around and stormed out of Doc Miller's Office, slamming the door behind him.

As Becker walked down the stairs to the street, he began talking to himself. He often talked to himself when he was angry. Right now he was angry with himself for not having the backbone to take Sam Willard into custody when he had the best chance he was probably ever going to get. He was also angry with Doc for his comment about hurting himself with his own gun.

By the time Becker reached the bottom of the stairs, he had almost talked himself into going back to Doc Miller's office and arresting Sam. He stopped and looked back up at the door to Doc's office. The only thing keeping him from going back up the stairs was the realization that if he tried to arrest Sam now, he might make Sam mad enough to kill him.

Becker also began to realize that if Sam didn't kill him, he would have the Willard Ranch hands to deal with as well as most of the town folks. The town folks would probably run him out of town on a rail like Doc said, and just when things were beginning to look up for him.

Sheriff Becker rationalized that Sam would eventually be taken care of by the small ranchers in the area. When the drought got bad enough, they would take care of Sam for him and he wouldn't have to lift a finger. That thought made him smile as he continued to think about what it might mean to him.

When the small ranchers band together and take over the Willard Ranch for its water, he would arrest the ranchers that killed Sam and take possession of the Willard Ranch. Having possession of the Willard Ranch would give him control of most of the water in the valley.

Once he had control of the water, he would have power over everyone in the valley, or at least most of the ranches in the valley. That would make him a very important man, as well as very rich. Something he would never be as the local sheriff.

With that thought firmly set in his mind, he returned to his office with a grin on his face. He was now feeling satisfied that everything would work out for him. He wasn't sure what it would take to make it work out in his favor, but he was confident it would even if he wasn't sure how.

Meanwhile, Sam sat in Doc Miller's office to rest for a moment and talk. Neither of them liked Becker. They both thought of him as a poor excuse for a sheriff, and an even poorer excuse for a human being. They also knew him to be a coward. If push came to shove, Becker would get someone else to do his dirty work, even if he had to hire it done.

"Sam, you need to watch your back around him. I wouldn't trust that little weasel as far as I could throw him. It would be just like him to shoot you in the back."

"I don't trust him, either. But I don't think he has the nerve to shoot a man, even in the back. He certainly doesn't have the nerve to shoot a man when he's facing him. He's more the type to get someone to do it for him," Sam replied.

"You really believe that, don't you?"

"Yes. Yes, I do. After all, hasn't it been tried already?"

"Yeah. I suppose you're right. But do you really think Becker hired those two men to kill you?" Doc Miller asked.

"There's no doubt in my mind Becker knew why they were in town. He may even have known who they were. Whether he actually hired them himself, I have my doubts. But I wouldn't be surprised if he knew who did. I think there is someone else involved in this, someone who thinks they have a lot to gain from seeing me dead. I'm sure Becker thinks he is going to be in on any gains made as a result of my death.

"I have a good idea who hired the bushwhackers, but I can't prove it," Sam said thoughtfully. "With both of those two hired guns dead, it will be impossible to prove anything."

"I tend to agree with you on that," Doc Miller said. "They will be taking the bodies over to the undertaker. I'll examine them there. I'll see what I can find out about them and let you know."

"Thanks Doc. I'd appreciate it. If you find out anything, it might be best if you keep it between us," Sam suggested.

"You can count on it. I would like to see Becker run out of town," Doc Miller added.

"I would, too," Sam agreed as he stood up. "I'd better be going. I have a lot to do. I'm going over to the Red Garter Saloon and see if Jake might have come up with something on them."

"You take care. You never know just what it takes to get a man's courage up until you've already pushed him too far. I think if Becker is pushed hard enough, he'll break. And when a man breaks, there's no telling what he'll try to do," Doc Miller warned Sam.

"You might be right, Doc. I'll keep that in mind. I'll be careful."

"One other thing, with Frank Gregory and Will Carter not liking you, it might not be safe for you to travel around the county alone."

"I'm beginning to agree with you," Sam assured him.

With that said, Sam started for the door. He hesitated at the door and looked around before stepping outside. All he could think of was this was the second time in as many days someone had tried to bushwhack him. This was a time for him to be on his guard and to be watchful of his surroundings. He was wishing he had taken Casey's advice and had a couple of his ranch hands ride into town with him.

CHAPTER FIVE

Sam started down the stairs from Doc Miller's office above Potter's General Store. His arm was a little sore and it was in a sling, but it wasn't giving him so much discomfort that he couldn't concentrate on what was going on around him. When he reached the bottom of the stairs, he stopped and looked up and down the street. He was being especially careful, but for good reason. He had no desire to walk into another scrap so soon.

Just as Sam was about to turn and head on down the street toward the Red Garter Saloon, he saw a buggy coming into town from the south. Realizing it was Frank Gregory and his granddaughter, Marie, Sam turned the other way. He quickly moved down the boardwalk in front of the general store to the door and ducked inside.

"Is there something I can help you with, Sam?"

Sam turned and looked at the storekeeper. He knew John Potter fairly well. He had been dealing with him ever since John had set up his store in Shallow Creek. John had always seemed like an honest man and had always been fair in his dealings with Sam.

"Ahh, no, not at the moment. I'm just looking around," Sam replied, not sure what to say.

"Okay. Let me know if I can help you with anything," John said with a smile, then went on about his business of inventorying his stock and preparing an order.

Sam nodded, then walked over near the window and looked out. He saw Frank Gregory stop his buggy in front of the Sheriff's Office and get out. He watched Frank tie the horse to the hitching rail.

Frank looked at the big black horse tied in front of the Sheriff's Office. He knew it belonged to Sam. He looked up and down the street looking for Sam, but didn't see him. A hint of a smile came over his face as if he already knew what had happened. He turned and talked to his granddaughter.

"I need to talk to Sheriff Becker for a minute. I'll meet you over at Potter's General Store."

"Will you be very long?"

"Long enough for you to look at the fabrics," he said as he smiled up at her.

Frank reached up and helped his granddaughter down from the buggy. He watched her as she walked toward the general store, then he turned and started toward the Sheriff's Office. At the door, he stopped and glanced at Marie as she went inside Potter's General Store. As he turned back toward the Sheriff's Office, he wondered if everything had gone well.

Sam was watching Marie as she crossed the
street, too. She was a pretty young woman. Her
dark brown hair flowed out from under her wide
brimmed bonnet. The dress she was wearing
showed off the smooth curves of her youthful figure.
She was one of those women that could catch a
man's eye and hold it.

Sam also noticed that Frank had stopped to
watch her cross the street. Sam stepped back away
from the window so Frank would not be able to see
him. He was sure if Frank saw him, he would not
allow Marie to come into the store.

As Sam waited in the corner for Marie to come
in, he wondered what Frank was planning on talking
to Becker about. He was sure it would have
something to do with the attack on him this
morning. It crossed his mind that Frank might be in
town to see how it went. It would not surprise Sam
if Gregory had been the one who hired the two
gunfighters, although he couldn't prove it. Sam let
that thought slip away as Marie entered the store.

"Marie," Sam said just loud enough for her to
hear as she closed the door.

"Sam," she replied with a slight tone of surprise
in her voice. "I saw your horse in front of the
Sheriff's Office. I wondered . . ."

Her surprise at seeing him quickly disappeared
when she saw his left arm was in a sling.

"What happened?" she asked as she quickly moved toward him.

"Nothing serious," he said as he watched her move across the room.

"Nothing serious? They don't put your arm in a sling for nothing serious. Tell me what happened?" she insisted.

Sam quickly realized it wouldn't do him any good to try to keep what had happened from her. It wouldn't be long and she would find out for herself. In fact, it wouldn't be long before the whole valley would know about the shootout in town.

Sam was also sure the story spread around would be told differently by different people and would eventually take on a life of its own. For example, there was no doubt in Sam's mind that the story told by Sheriff Becker would not be a very accurate account of what had actually happened. Sam was convinced Becker would make sure it sounded as if Sam had gunned down two innocent men in cold blood.

"A couple of men tried to bushwhack me when I came into town to see the sheriff."

"What reason would anyone have to want to kill you?" she asked in a sweet innocent tone as if she didn't believe him.

"For water, Marie."

"Water?"

"Yes, water. I have it and a lot of folks don't."

"But that's not your fault," she said as she fluttered her eyelashes at him.

"No. It's not. But there are some folks around here that wouldn't agree with you."

"That doesn't make sense."

"Oh, I agree. But there are still some who think it is my fault. There are a few people who are spreading the rumor that I have damned up the streams and creeks on my property to keep all the water for myself."

"Well, have you?" she asked in her shy innocent way.

Sam stared at her for a couple of seconds. He couldn't believe she would even ask such a question of him. He certainly would expect it from her grandfather or the sheriff, even from Will Carter, but not from her. It hurt him deeply that she had even asked. In fact, it made him angry.

"NO, I haven't," he replied sharply, his anger rising within him. "It would be my guess your grandfather has told you that I damned up the streams. Am I right?"

"Yes, he did say something about it to me. He said Mr. Carter told him that he had seen the dams and you had guards protecting them."

"Well, it's not true."

"What part is not true? The part about the dams, or the part about the guards?"

"None of it's true, but I guess you would think that way. For your information, Carter is a liar and so is your grandfather. It's my guess the sheriff is one of those who has been helping to spread the lies, too," he said growing more and more frustrated with Marie's apparent lack of understanding.

"I suppose you think the sheriff hired those men who tried to kill you?" she asked, her voice indicating she had already decided who she was going to believe.

"I don't know, but I think he is involved in some way. I just haven't figured out how."

"My grandfather is over at the Sheriff's Office right now."

"I know. I saw you come into town," Sam replied as he looked at her wondering where her train of thought was going.

"Do you have any idea who it was that tried to kill you?"

Sam wasn't sure why she would ask such a question. He wondered if her interest was casual, or if she wanted to know for some other reason. He began to think anything he told her would be passed on to her grandfather. He felt the need to be very careful about what he said.

"No, but I will eventually find out who they were. I will also find out who hired them," he answered with a determined tone to his voice.

The fact that Sam seemed so determined to find out who was trying to kill him, along with the angry look on his face, worried her. Marie didn't want anything to happen to Sam. In spite of what her grandfather thought of him, she sort of liked him. Of course, the fact he owned the biggest ranch in the valley and was the wealthiest rancher in the valley did a lot to improve her feelings for him. To Marie this made him the most eligible man around, and she wanted him, and his ranch.

"Oh, I wish all this wasn't happening. I wish it would just go away," she said, the tone of her voice showing how unpleasant all the talk about shootings, killings and range wars was for her.

"I wish it wasn't happening, either. But the fact remains it is happening. You can't bury your head in the sand and hope it will just go away, because it won't."

"It's just so, oh, I don't know, so ugly," she said as she wrinkled up her face to show how much she disliked the thought of it all.

"Well, unless we get a good deal of rain pretty soon, there will be a lot more blood shed around here. And there will be very little anyone will be able to do to stop it," Sam said with a note of frustration.

Sam was growing frustrated with her for her apparent inability to face up to the realities of the situation. He couldn't help but think she was acting more like a spoiled little brat, and not like the grown woman she was supposed to be.

"Couldn't you maybe help get water to your neighbors?" she asked, obviously unable to understand the difficulty and the expense of such an undertaking.

"And just how am I supposed to do that?"

"I don't know," she replied softly, her expression suggesting she wished she had not mentioned it and that the whole discussion was very depressing to her.

"I hardly have enough water to keep my own cattle alive, much less the rest of the herds in the valley. Besides, water isn't the only problem. The grazing land is drying up, too. If it doesn't rain soon we won't have enough grass to feed the cattle."

As Sam watched her, he saw the expression on Marie's face suddenly change. He had also noticed she was not paying any attention to him. It was as if what he was saying was boring her. Her attention had turned to something else, something outside. He wondered what it was she found more interesting or more important than listening to him.

"What is it?" Sam asked.

"My grandfather's coming," she replied casually. "I don't think it would be a good idea if he saw us talking."

Marie reached out and took his hand. She looked up at him. He could see something in her eyes, but he was not sure what it was. Could it be she cared for him, or was she trying to avoid a confrontation with her grandfather? He thought she might be torn between how she felt for him and her loyalty to her grandfather, which was something he could understand.

"I'll slip out the back," Sam said casually as he let go of her hand.

The last thing Sam wanted was to get into a confrontation with her grandfather. It wouldn't do either of them any good.

"That's probably best. When will I see you again?" she asked.

"I don't know," he replied as if he wasn't interested in talking about it.

After what Marie had said, along with her attitude, Sam wasn't sure how he felt about her anymore. He wasn't even sure if he cared if he saw her again. There was something about the way she acted that made him question his interest in her. She didn't seem to comprehend what was going on around her. It was as if she found it so distasteful she was simply going to shut it out of her mind so it wouldn't continue to distress her. He got the impression it was all a big inconvenience to her and she was unable to grasp the seriousness of the situation.

"We could meet at the big oak tree on Stone Creek where our property lines join tomorrow evening," she said almost as if it was a second thought.

Sam looked at her as she started to move away from him. The fact she asked him if he had damned up the creeks and streams left him thinking about how much she really cared about him. He had this gut feeling she was after something from him, but he wasn't sure what it could be.

"What time?" he finally replied, almost not caring if he met with her or not.

"About nine o'clock," she said as she motioned for him to get out of sight.

Sam had no more than ducked out of sight when he heard the bell on the front door of the store ring. He knew it was Frank coming in to get Marie. He stopped and leaned up against the wall out of sight to listen.

"I think we should go home," Frank said as he walked up to Marie.

The tone of Frank's voice was sharp making his comment sound more like an order than a suggestion. He seemed to be in a hurry. The look on his face showed he was not very happy about something.

"But I haven't finished looking," Marie said as she turned around to face her grandfather.

"You can look some other time. I think we should leave now," he insisted.

"What is the hurry?" she asked.

"I think we should leave now," he insisted again, only more firmly.

"I want to know why?" she asked, again sounding like a spoiled child.

Frank looked at her. He didn't like the way she was acting, but he didn't want to alienate his granddaughter, either. He also didn't want to cause a scene in front of Mr. Potter who was watching them from behind the counter.

"Sam Willard is in town and he just killed two men," Frank said sharply as he watched her for a reaction.

"I have already heard about it," she said looking him in the eyes.

"Becker told me that he gunned down two men in the middle of the street for no reason," he said.

"Are you sure?" she asked, acting as if she was no longer sure who she should believe.

"Yes. Becker would not lie to me," Frank insisted.

"Those two men probably tried to kill Sam," she said as she turned away from her grandfather and glanced toward the back of the store.

"You've seen Willard, haven't you?"

"Yes," she admitted as she turned back around to face her grandfather.

"What makes you so sure he is telling the truth?"

"He wouldn't lie to me," she replied holding her head up high.

"Well, no granddaughter of mine is going to have anything to do with the likes of Willard. We're going home and now."

"Grandpa, don't you see what is happening here?"

"Yes, I do. Willard is hoarding all the water in an effort to drive us out of the valley."

"I don't think he is trying to do that. Can't you see, he needs the same things you need? He needs for it to rain so the grass can grow, and so the streams and creeks will run with water again. So the watering holes on all the ranches in the valley can be full of water again," she said as she glanced toward the back of the store.

"He has water. He's damned up the streams. That's why there is no water in the creeks and streams for the rest of us."

"I don't think he would do that to his neighbors," Marie said a little louder hoping Sam could still hear her.

"And just how do you know that?"

"I don't, but I don't think he is the kind of man who would do that. He's a good man," she said, taking a quick glance toward the back of the store.

"I'm going home. Are you coming?"

Frank stood and looked at his granddaughter for a moment or two before he turned around and started out the door. Marie looked at him and let out a sigh of disappointment that she could not change his mind. There was no doubt in her mind that he would leave without her so she followed him as far as the door.

She stopped briefly at the front door of the store and looked back toward where Sam had disappeared earlier. Marie couldn't see if he was still there. She wondered if Sam had heard her conversation with her grandfather. She hoped he had heard it. It would put her in good standing with him, something she wanted very much. She smiled to herself as she turned and followed her grandfather across the street.

As she followed him toward the buggy, Marie silently wished her grandfather would see things the way she did. She wasn't ready to tell her grandfather about her plans to get Sam to marry her, not yet anyway. She would wait for a better time to tell him, when he wasn't so upset.

If she could persuade her grandfather to at least pretend to like Sam, even a little bit; she was convinced she could talk Sam into marrying her. Then the two ranches could become one and her grandfather would not have to work another day in his life. They could both enjoy the kind of lifestyle wealth could bring. The kind of lifestyle she knew her grandfather had enjoyed in the South before the Great War.

To Marie's way of thinking it didn't hurt that Sam was handsome as well as wealthy. He could give her a good heir to the ranch.

Marie got to the buggy just as Frank was ready to get in. He looked at her. It was easy to see that he was angry with her, but if her plan worked he would be proud of her and all would be forgiven.

Marie got into the buggy and sat down. When Frank turned the buggy around and headed out of town, she glanced over her shoulder and looked toward Potter's General Store. A smile of satisfaction came over her face as she thought about Sam and his ranch, and how some day she would have control of both.

CHAPTER SIX

Sam had remained out of sight in the back of Potter's General Store. Although he could not see Marie and her grandfather, he could hear them talking. He listened very carefully to their discussion. Sam still wasn't sure if Marie really believed him, or if she simply wanted him to think she did. There was something about the way she spoke to her grandfather that left Sam's mind cluttered with doubts about her.

As soon as Marie followed her grandfather out of the store, Sam slipped out the back of the general store. He quickly moved around to the side of the building and watched as the buggy left town with Marie sitting beside her grandfather.

Marie was sitting with her back straight and as ridged as a ramrod. Sam saw her turn and glance toward the front of the general store. She had a smile on her face. When she turned back around, he wondered what was going on in her mind. Was the smile meant for him, or was she pleased with herself for some reason he didn't understand?

As soon as the buggy was out of sight, Sam leaned up against the side of the building and let out a long sigh. He took a minute to think about what had happen between them in the general store. At this point, he wasn't sure how he felt about Marie. He wasn't even sure if she would meet him at the large oak tree tomorrow night.

Marie's apparent lack of interest in what was going on in the valley, and the fact she didn't seem to want to believe him, made him doubt if she really cared for him at all. If that was the case, what was she after? What did she really want? The more he thought about it, the more he wasn't sure if he wanted to meet her at the oak tree.

After a few minutes, Sam's thoughts turned back to Jake and what had happened earlier behind the Red Garter Saloon. He began to slowly walk along behind the buildings as he tried to put everything that had happened into perspective.

When he arrived at the back of the saloon, he stopped and looked down at the blood in the dirt. The bodies of the two men were gone now, but there were still signs of what had taken place there. Sam assumed the bodies had been taken over to the undertaker's office or over to Doc Miller's office while he was in the general store.

Sam looked up at the backdoor of the saloon. He still felt the need to talk to Jake. He reached for the door handle. Just as his hand was about to touch it, the door swung opened. Sam reached down and quickly drew his gun. It was in his hand and pointed toward the door before it was open.

"Whoa," Jake said as he raised his hands to show he was unarmed.

"Sorry, Jake. I guess I'm a little jumpy," Sam said as he slid his gun back into his holster in one smooth motion.

"Hell, I don't blame you, but don't shoot me."

"I wouldn't shoot you. I was coming over to see what you might have found out about those two men."

"I was going out to the shed to get a couple of things, but it can wait. Come on in," Jake suggested. "You look like you could use a beer."

Jake didn't wait for a response from Sam. He simply turned around and went back inside the saloon. Sam followed him. Once inside, Jake went around behind the bar, poured a beer and offered it to Sam.

"You could probably use this," he said as he held out the beer for Sam.

"Thanks," Sam replied, then stepped up to the bar and accepted the beer.

"To answer your question, I really don't know anything about those two fellas," Jake said as he poured himself a beer.

"When did they get into town?"

"I don't rightly know for sure. The first time I saw them was shortly before six o'clock last night. They came in here and ordered dinner. From the looks of them, I'd have to say they'd been riding pretty hard for some time to get here."

"Any idea why they would have ridden so hard?"

"Nope. Nobody I know rides that hard for anything less than money," Jake said with a grin.

"Did they ask for anyone, or seem to know anyone around here?"

"Nope."

"Did they talk to anyone?"

"I didn't see them talking to anyone. It was kind of slow in here last night. Becker came by a couple of times, but that ain't unusual for him."

"Was there anything to indicate they might have known him, or that he knew them?" Sam asked hoping for something that would give him a clue as to who had put them up to shooting him.

Jake sipped his beer while he took a minute to try to recall what it was he had seen last night. He then set his beer down on the bar and looked at Sam.

"I don't recall seeing anything that would indicate Becker knew them, or they knew him for that matter. Sorry."

"Have you seen either of them before?"

"Not to my recollection."

Sam sipped his beer as he tried to think. He was disappointed that he was not able to find out who they were or anything about them. It was too bad they had both been killed, but under the circumstances it couldn't have been helped.

"Has Becker been over here to talk to you about them, or about the shooting?"

"No, not really," Jake replied, wondering what Sam was getting at.

"That's strange," Sam said thoughtfully as he set his beer down on the bar.

Jake could see by the expression on Sam's face that he was thinking very hard about something.

"What's on your mind, Sam?"

"Follow me on this. There's been a shooting in town and you're involved. Becker doesn't even come and talk to you about it."

"He talked to me after it happened out in back. In fact, it was shortly after you left for Doc Miller's Office."

"Yeah, but he was over at Doc's a few minutes after I got there wanting to arrest me for killing them. He couldn't have talked to you for more than a minute or so."

"That's true enough," Jake agreed. "He asked me who shot the men, I told him you shot one and I shot the other, then he left."

"But nothing else?"

"Nope. He didn't even ask what happened, or what it was all about."

"That's my point, he didn't ask you what happened."

"No, he didn't," Jake replied, still not understanding what Sam was getting at.

"He didn't ask you about what happened because he didn't have to. He didn't try to arrest you for killing one of them, did he?"

"No, he didn't," Jake replied as he continued to listen to Sam.

"He wanted to arrest me for killing them, but didn't want to arrest you after you made it clear that you had killed one of them. Doesn't that strike you as a little strange?"

Jake looked at Sam as he thought about what Sam had said. Now that it had been put that way, it did seem a little strange to Jake.

"It's strange, all right. But I don't get what you're getting at, Sam?"

"It would seem to me that if any sheriff worth his salt had a shooting in his town, he would investigate and find out who shot who and why. It would seem to me that he would at least make an effort to find out who they were and why they were here. Wouldn't you think?"

"Yeah. I see your point."

"What reason would Becker have for not coming over here and at least talking to you about those two, even asking some of the same questions I asked?" Sam asked in an effort to get Jake to think a little harder about it.

"Because he already knew who they were and why they were here?" Jake asked.

"That's right. Becker knew those two and why they were here."

"Why would Becker want you dead? I know he doesn't like you, but what would he have to gain from seeing you dead?"

"That's a good question. Especially since I frankly don't think Becker is the one who hired them to kill me."

"You just said Becker knew all about it," Jake said looking a little confused.

"Yes, he knew about it. But I don't think he hired those two. There has to be someone else behind this, someone with the money to pay for two gunfighters."

"Who?" Jake asked.

"It could be any one of several people I can think of, but I don't know which one."

"Who do you think it might be?"

"I'd rather not say until I'm sure. I don't want to start a bunch of rumors."

"What are you going to do about it?"

"I don't know. I want you to keep this conversation between us. I don't want anyone to know what we talked about."

"No problem, Sam. I won't say anything."

"Good. By the way, I want to thank you for saving my life."

"You're welcome, Sam. Besides, I don't cotton to back shooters."

"I, for one, am very glad of that. If there is anything I can do for you, just let me know."

"I don't need nothin'. I'll tell you this, though. I'll keep my eyes and ears open from now on. If I see or hear anything, I'll get word to you."

"I'd appreciate that, Jake."

Sam lifted his glass and drank down the remainder of the beer. He set the glass on the bar and started for the front door.

"You be careful out there," Jake said as Sam reached the door.

Jake's comment came as a warning that Sam was not about to ignore. He stopped at the swinging doors and looked out onto the street. It was getting on toward noon. The sun was high in the clear sky, and it was getting hot. He noticed there were now several people milling around town, each of them going about his own business.

Across the street where he had left his horse, Sam could see Becker sitting on a chair in front of his office. He didn't seem at all concerned that there had been a shooting in town. The more Sam thought about it, the more convinced he became that Becker was somehow involved. The only questions were how was he involved and who was he involved with?

Once satisfied the street was safe to cross, Sam stepped out of the saloon onto the boardwalk. He took both Jake's and Doc Miller's warnings serious.

He checked up and down the street before he stepped out into the street.

Once he was in the street, Sam stepped lively while still keeping his eyes on Becker. He saw Becker sit up straight in the chair. As long as Becker stayed in the chair, he was not in a position to draw his gun, but Sam was ready just the same.

Becker watched every step Sam took as he walked across the street toward his horse. He was angry, it could be seen in his eyes and in the way he watched Sam.

Sam walked up beside his horse making sure to keep his horse between Becker and himself. Becker stood up and watched Sam closely. Sam knew he would be in the worst possible position to defend himself when he put his foot in the stirrup and started to swing up into the saddle. To be on the safe side, Sam simply untied his horse and started leading him down the street. He kept his horse between them until he reached the corner of the building. Sam then turned and led his horse around the corner. Once he was out of Becker's sight, he put his foot in the stirrup and swung himself into the saddle as quickly as possible.

Without a moment's hesitation, he firmly kicked the horse with his spurs and rode off at a fast gallop. Sam wanted to put as much distance between him and the town as he could in case someone else was out to get him.

Once the little town of Shallow Creek was behind him and out of sight, Sam let his horse settle into a nice smooth gallop that covered a lot of ground in a short time. It was an easy gait for the big horse. It gave Sam time to think, and one of the things he thought about was what he needed to do to protect his ranch.

One of the things he decided was to have none of his ranch hands ride alone while out on the range checking cattle and watering holes. He would have his ranch hands always ride in pairs, even if it took only one ranch hand do the job.

Another was to keep a steady watch on the ranch house, the barns, and especially his supply of feed for his cattle. He needed to keep that area of the ranch guarded and secure. If necessary, the ranch house and barns could become a fortress. That part of the ranch would be fairly easy to defend, if need be.

As Sam rode along toward his ranch, his thoughts turned to Marie. He had been disappointed that she had listened and believed her grandfather. It was not hard for him to understand why she would believe whatever her grandfather told her. After all, he had raised her since she was a small child. For many years she had looked up to him.

It had not been Sam's intention to make Marie take sides, but it appeared to be what was happening. After giving it some serious thought, he began to realize that the differences between her grandfather and him was putting her in a position where she might very well have to choose between them before this was over. He had never wanted that to happen.

It was bad enough that there were bad feelings between Frank and him, but to have to drag her into it was making Sam feel like it would be best if he just dropped out of the picture as far as Marie was concerned. Besides, he wasn't sure that there was anything between them they could build a lasting relationship on anyway.

That thought did not set well with Sam. He liked Marie from the first time he saw her as a grown woman. She seemed to like him and he knew she was not seeing anyone else. There was no doubt she was the prettiest woman Sam could remember seeing in some time. Up until today he had thought she was smart, but his talk with her this morning had made him wonder about that.

The only one standing in his way of pursuing her was her grandfather. Yet, Sam had this strange feeling that he might not want to pursue her anymore. He had seen a side to her today that he had not seen before, and he didn't care for it. Any woman who was going to share his life had to understand what it took to run a large ranch like the Willard Ranch. She had to understand that when problems came around, they had to be dealt with.

They couldn't be simply ignored and hope they went away. To Sam's way of thinking, Marie did not fit the bill.

Sam couldn't put his finger on it, but there was a little voice in the back of his head telling him that she was not all she seemed to be. At times she was almost like a child, then there were times when she seemed to be hard and cold.

Sam was slowly coming to the realization that Marie wanted something from him, but he was not sure what it was. Whatever it was, she wanted it more than she wanted him.

The only thing Sam could think of that Marie might want more than him was his ranch. He wondered if she might believe that being Mrs. Samuel Willard would give her some sort of status in the valley. Being Mrs. Samuel Willard would certainly make her the wife of the richest man in the valley. He felt she might believe that alone would give her the kind of prestige she had when she was living on her grandfather's plantation before the war. Sam tried to dismiss that thought, but he could not clear it from his head easily.

He questioned if his thoughts about her were based on gut feelings. or if his mind was telling him to be careful. With all that had happened in town, he was not sure what to think. He decided he would try not to think about Marie until things cooled down a little in the valley, which could take some time. Then he would try to take a good look at their relationship and see if there was anything to it.

CHAPTER SEVEN

Sam's big horse had covered the ground back to the ranch in good time and without any more problems. As Sam turned and rode up the lane to the ranch house, he could see Casey pacing back and forth on the front pouch. Casey looked as if he was waiting impatiently for him to return.

Sam's first thought was that Casey was worried about his safety, but he knew Casey would not simply stand around all morning waiting for him to return. He would still do the job expected of him, and he would do it without complaint. There had to be something else troubling Casey. From the look on Casey's face, Sam knew something was not right.

Casey heard Sam coming up the lane. He stopped pacing and turned to watch Sam as he rode toward the ranch house.

"Good to see yah back, boss," Casey said.

"Good to be back."

"Say, what happened to yah?" Casey asked when he noticed the sling on Sam's arm.

"I had a little run-in in town. Nothing serious."

"That's good," Casey replied without asking for further details.

"What's going on?" Sam asked as he stepped out of the saddle.

"Johnny ain't come back from his rounds of the waterin' holes in the south pasture. He shoulda been back hours ago. I'm worried about him."

"That's not like him. Did he go out alone?"

"Sure, just like always" Casey replied, wondering why Sam would even ask such a question.

Sam tied his horse to the hitching rail in front of the house then stepped up on the porch next to Casey. The news of Johnny not returning worried him, too. Johnny had always been a dependable, hard working ranch hand. It was not like him.

"Have you sent anyone out to look for him?" Sam asked as he turned and looked out across the open rangeland hoping to see Johnny come riding in.

"Yeah. I sent three of the hands out to look for him. They should be back soon."

"From now on I don't want anyone riding alone. Always send the men out in pairs, at least."

"You expectin' more trouble, boss?"

"I sure am. Someone hired a couple of gunfighters to gun me down in town. If it hadn't of been for Jake, they might have succeeded."

"I told yah that yah shoulda taken a couple of the hands with yah," Casey reminded Sam.

"That you did. I guess you were right, Casey."

Just then Sam straightened up and turned to look off toward a distant hill. He had caught a glimpse of several riders coming over the top of the hill. They were headed toward the ranch house and moving kind of slow. Casey turned and looked, too.

"Looks like the hands are coming back," Sam said.

"Yeah, and it looks like they might've run inta some trouble," Casey said as he watched the riders approach.

"Looks like they've got someone over a saddle," Sam said as he stepped down off the porch and waited for the men to ride into the ranch yard.

As the men rode into the yard, Sam could see it was Johnny slung over the saddle. Sam's first reaction was disappointment. He had hoped Johnny would be found unharmed.

Johnny had been a good ranch hand. He worked hard and did his job without complaint. It was no way for such a fine young man to end up. The riders reined up in front of the ranch house and looked at Sam.

"Sorry, boss," one of the riders said not knowing what else to say under the circumstances.

"Got any idea what happened out there?" Sam asked as he looked up at the lead rider.

"Don't know for sure, boss. We found him laying at the edge of one of the watering holes over near the south fork of Musk Creek. He'd been shot in the back, twice. His gun was still in his holster. He never had a chance," the ranch hand said.

Sam could hear the anger in the man's voice and he could feel the anger growing inside himself. Johnny had become the first victim in what was promising to be a full-blown, all out range war, if someone didn't do something to put a stop to it quickly.

There was no doubt Sam's men were ready to go out, find the killer and string him up on the first tree they found big enough to hang a man on. Sam was in favor of the idea except for one problem. The problem was they didn't know who to string up.

"Take him over to the ice house and have Davy make him a coffin. We'll bury him first thing in the morning," Sam instructed his men.

"Boss, we think we should pay a visit to old man Gregory," one of the ranch hands said.

"You got reason to think Gregory shot Johnny?"

"Not really," the ranch hand admitted after giving it some thought. "But with the way he's been talkin', I'd be willin' to bet it was him."

"I'm inclined to agree with you, but do you have any proof? You can't hang a man for talking."

Sam was almost wishing the ranch hand had some kind of proof. If he had any proof, it might make it possible to put a stop to all the shooting and violence. It would also provide some justice for the killing of Johnny.

"No," the ranch hand admitted softly.

"If you've got proof, I'll be the first one to go after him."

"I ain't got no proof, boss. I'm sorry I opened my big mouth."

"It's okay. I understand how you feel. I feel the same. But I don't want anyone taking matters into their own hands. At this point, we don't know who shot Johnny. And until we do, we don't do anything. You understand?" Sam said, his voice carrying the sound of authority.

The ranch hands, still sitting on their horses, looked at one another then turned back toward the boss. They all nodded they understood even if they didn't necessarily agree.

"I want you to take care of Johnny and then get your horses put up. After you've finished your chores and had dinner, I want everyone to come up here to the house. We are going to have a talk and make plans so this sort of thing doesn't happen again," Sam said.

"Okay, yah heard the boss," Casey said stepping forward. "Get a move on."

Sam watched as the men turned their horses and slowly rode toward the corral. He could understand the men's feelings. All of them liked Johnny.

"Casey, come inside. We need to have a talk before we meet with the men."

"Sure, boss."

Casey followed Sam into the house. Once inside, Sam pointed to a chair for Casey to sit in.

"Casey, I think we're in for a long hot summer," Sam said as he sat down in a chair close to Casey.

"I'm sure you're right, boss."

"I know that Frank Gregory didn't kill Johnny. I saw him in town this morning."

"Maybe not. But if he hired the man who did shoot Johnny, then he's as guilty as the man who done it."

"I won't argue with you on that."

"What are we going to do about it?" Casey asked, looking to his boss for answers.

"I don't know yet. The one thing we are not going to do is to go off half-cocked. Too many people get hurt that way. I want Johnny's killer as much as you or any of the other men, but I want the right person hung for it. If we hang the wrong person, then we're no better than the person who shot him."

Casey nodded that he agreed with Sam's assessment. The one thing that bothered Casey was he knew that Sam liked Marie, Frank Gregory's granddaughter. He felt Frank was more than likely responsible for Johnny's death. Casey had to wonder if Sam's feeling for Marie might cloud his judgment a little. He wondered if he should say something to Sam about it. He decided he would not say anything right now, but that didn't mean he wouldn't say something in the future.

In spite of his concerns, Casey would do as he was told. He rode for the brand. That meant whatever happened, he would be on the side of his boss.

"First thing in the morning we're going to get Johnny laid to rest. We'll bury him up by the old cottonwood tree on the hill. Then you and I are going to have a couple of the men take us out to where they found Johnny. We're going to see if we can find anything that might lead us to who shot him. I don't want anyone talking about this to anyone outside this ranch. You understand?"

"Yes, sir."

"I don't want anyone leaving the ranch and going into town. At least for the time being, the town is off limits. It would be too easy for the men to get into trouble. Sheriff Becker is looking for any excuse at all to put one or two of my men in jail, or shoot them. I don't want to give him the chance."

"I understand. I'm sure they'll understand," Casey said as he stood up.

"One more thing. Check with the men and see if any of them know of anyone who has and uses a 40-60 caliber rifle.

"Will do," Casey said, then turned and left the ranch house.

As soon as Casey left, Sam went out to the kitchen. Margaret Dunberry, a rather large woman who had been cooking and cleaning for Sam for the past few years, offered him a hot cup of coffee. As he took the cup from her, he noticed tears in her eyes.

"What's the matter, Margaret?" he asked, although he was sure he already knew.

"I'm goin' to miss that young man. He was always willing to help me by gettin' wood for the stove and things like that."

"We're all going to miss him."

"What's goin' on with people, Mr. Willard?"

Sam could hear the frustration in her voice, and her need for answers. In fact, they all had a need for answers.

"What do you mean?"

"You've been shot at twice, Johnny's been killed and there's talk of a range war. What's wrong with people?"

"I guess people do funny things when they're under a lot of stress."

"I don't find it funny, Mr. Willard," she said with a shocked look on her face.

"I didn't mean funny like that, I meant more like people do strange things, even stupid things. Things they normally wouldn't do."

"Oh, I'm sorry," she replied, a little embarrassed that she had not understood his meaning.

"That's all right. I wish things were not the way they are, but there is very little I can do to change them. When people get jealous of others, they sometimes don't think like they should," Sam said in an effort to explain what was happening.

"I guess I'll never understand people," she replied as she shook her head.

"I guess I won't either," Sam said with a sigh.

"I'll get your dinner ready, Mr. Willard," she said as she turned back toward the woodstove.

Sam sat at the table thinking when Margaret brought him his dinner. He knew Margaret didn't understand what was happening, but then he didn't fully understand it either. It seemed so senseless for people to fight over something they could do nothing about.

There was no doubt the rain would come again. The streams and creeks would run full, the watering holes would be full and the prairie would be green again. This would all happen, but only when the rains were ready to spread out over the land. Fighting among themselves would not solve anything or help anyone, and it certainly wouldn't bring the much needed rain.

After Sam had finished his dinner, he went out and sat on the front porch. It was getting on near dusk when he saw the men coming toward the ranch house. The one thing he had to do was to keep his men from getting out of control and doing something they would regret later.

Once the shock of Johnny's death wore off, anger would set in amongst the men. If he was to keep his men under control, he needed to keep a cool head himself.

Casey gathered the men around the front porch of the ranch house. As they stood around, they listened to Sam as he explained what was happening and why, at least, as best he could.

The men seemed to understand what was going on. Most of them had at least heard about range wars, even if they had not actively been caught up in one. It was clear some of the men wanted to do something about Johnny's death right now, but they really didn't know what to do. It was mostly the anger in them doing the thinking at the moment. Sam had to help them get past it.

After a while, the men seemed to understand where Sam was coming from. They really didn't want to take their anger out on the wrong person. Sam explained that if they did, they would be no better than those who had killed Johnny.

Sam didn't feel he had to tell his men why he wanted them to travel in pairs, or why he wanted them to be on guard at all times. Johnny's death would be reminder enough. The one thing he didn't want to have to do was to bury another of his ranch hands.

After Sam finished explaining things to his men, he gave any of them who wanted it a chance to leave.

"Now, any of you who don't wish to stay here and fight for the ranch are free to collect your pay and leave. No one here will blame you if you choose to leave. You were not hired to be gunfighters. You were hired to work a ranch."

Sam stood quietly and looked over his men as he waited to see if any of them were going to leave. Casey was looking at them, too.

"I don't think anyone wants ta leave, boss," Casey said, proud of the men for sticking with the boss.

"Thank you all for sticking with me. Effective right now, I don't want to see anyone working alone. If the job requires only one man, the other is to stay close and keep his eyes open, sort of cover each other's back. If the job takes two men, I want a third man standing by and watching for trouble. And those of you working, keep your guns close by and ready to use. I expect you to protect yourselves and each other at all times.

"In fact, I want you all to keep your eyes open and report anything or anybody you see that doesn't belong on this ranch to Casey or to me. I don't want you taking matters into your own hands.

"Never go anywhere without a gun that isn't ready to use. And that includes going from the bunkhouse to the dining hall," Sam added. "Any questions?"

After waiting a moment or two without getting any questions, Sam thanked his men again for sticking with him, then turned them over to Casey.

Casey told the men they could return to what they were doing, then followed several of them toward the bunkhouse. A couple of the men took up their positions as guards, one near the barn and one near the haystacks.

Sam knew tomorrow would be a busy day. He went inside the house and sat down at his desk in the corner of the living room. He began to think about Johnny and how he had been killed.

Remembering what he had told Casey about seeing Frank Gregory and Marie in town, he began to think about it. He remembered that Frank and Marie had not arrived in Shallow Creek until well after he had been in the shoot-out. Johnny had left on his rounds of the watering holes almost before sunrise. He had been found at one of the first places he would have checked. Frank would have had plenty of time to have killed Johnny and still made it to town to meet with Sheriff Becker.

Sam leaned back in his chair while he thought about it. Sam began to wonder if Frank's visit to Sheriff Becker had been to tell him that he had killed one of Sam's ranch hands, or to find out if the hired guns had killed him. Maybe both.

If Frank had killed Johnny, or had him killed, Sam would want him to pay for it. Sam felt it might not happen unless he got some outside help. The Territorial Marshal would be the logical person to help find and put Johnny's killer away.

It was getting late and Sam had to be up early. He decided he would sleep on it for the night and make his decision on what he should do in the morning, after they took care of Johnny.

CHAPTER EIGHT

Chores always start early on a ranch and the Willard Ranch was no exception. Before the ranch hands would begin their chores, they had to be fed, and fed well for the work on a ranch was hard. The cook's day always started well before the rest. It was the cook's job to make sure the ranch hands had good food and plenty of it.

Sam was up before the sun, which was his usual practice. His left arm was still a little sore and stiff, but that was about all. The dressing over the wound was clean and dry. He needed to get to work and he knew the sling was going to be in the way. He decided against using the sling and would try to go about his business without it.

Sam's first order of business today was to put Johnny Marsh in his final resting place. His second order of business was going out to where Johnny had been shot in the hope of finding out who had killed him, or at least find some evidence leading to his killer.

Sam went out to the kitchen where a warm breakfast was waiting for him. He took a sip of hot coffee before saying anything to Margaret who was busy making breakfast for the rest of the ranch hands.

"Good morning, Margaret," he said as he set his cup down.

"Good morning, Mr. Willard. I heard you tell some of the men that you would be going out to where Johnny was killed this morning. Will you be going soon?"

"After we take care of Johnny," Sam answered solemnly.

"Mr. Willard, did Johnny have any kin folks?"

"None I know of, Margaret. I thought we'd bury him up on the hill next to the old cottonwood tree. What do you think about it?"

Margaret looked at Sam. She was a little surprised he was interested in her opinion on where Johnny should be laid to rest. He had never asked her for her opinion on anything other than on what was served to the men for meals. That simple gesture showed her that even though he was her boss, he valued her opinion.

"I think it would be a nice place. It's a pretty spot. I'll pick some wild flowers this afternoon and put them on his grave, if you don't mind," Margaret said, her voice showing the sadness she was feeling in her heart.

"I think that would be very nice. You be sure to take a couple of the men with you when you go."

"Yes, sir," she replied as she returned to her work on the woodstove.

Sam didn't say anything more. He busied himself with finishing his breakfast. Margaret didn't say anything more, either. She simply continued her work even though she could not get Johnny off her mind.

When Sam finished his breakfast, he got up and went outside. He met up with Casey about half way across the yard to the icehouse.

"Mornin' boss."

"Morning Casey. Are we ready to take Johnny to his resting place?"

"Yes, sir. One of the hands asked me if it would be okay if he was to say a few words over Johnny after we put him in the ground and before we cover him up. Would that be okay with you, boss?" Casey asked.

"Sure. Who is it?"

"Doug. He and Johnny sorta partnered up whenever they got the chance. They was good friends."

"That would be fine, Casey."

As they walked together across the yard, Sam looked around. He saw one of the men leaning against the corner of the barn. He had a rifle held loosely in his hands and he was resting it across his legs. Although he looked as if he was very relaxed, Sam could tell by the way his head keep moving as he looked around that he was alert and ready for almost anything.

Sam turned to look toward the haystacks and saw another ranch hand standing guard there. If rain didn't come soon the hay could mean the difference between having his cattle survive or having to sell them off before they were ready for market. The haystacks had to be protected.

Once Sam and Casey got to the icehouse, Sam saw the coffin Davy had made for Johnny. It was laid across two sawhorses. It wasn't anything very pretty as coffins go, but it was made from what they had and Sam was sure Johnny would have approved. Davy had rather crudely carved Johnny's name in the top of the coffin.

Sam saw several of the ranch hands standing around waiting for things to get started. They were there to carry Johnny to his resting place and to bid him a final farewell.

Sam looked off toward the east. He could see the sun was just starting to lighten up the eastern sky. It was going to be another bright sunny day with few clouds and not much of a breeze to cool the day. It would be another day that would continue to dry up the watering holes and the creeks, and continue to dry up what little grass was left.

"I guess we better get started," Sam said as he looked at Casey.

"Yes, sir," Casey replied, then stepped toward the door to the icehouse.

Casey and two of the other men went inside the icehouse and brought Johnny's body out. They carefully placed him in the wooden coffin and crossed his arms over his chest. Everyone took one last look at Johnny before Davy and Casey placed the coffin lid over him and began nailing it closed.

As soon as it was nailed shut, several of the men lifted the coffin up on their shoulders. With a nod from Sam, they started off up the hill to the spot where he would be buried. Sam led the way while his men walked along behind. Everyone carried a rifle as well as side arms, except those carrying the coffin. The ones carrying the coffin had only side arms. They didn't really expect trouble, but they were ready for it just in case.

When they reached the top of the hill near the tree, they set the coffin down on the ground. They took ropes and slowly lowered Johnny's coffin into the hole a couple of the men had prepared the night before. All the men stood around the grave and listened while Sam read a passage from the Good Book he felt was appropriate.

After Doug said a few words about Johnny and recited a brief prayer his mother had taught him when he was a child. Each man in turn tossed a shovel full of dirt into the grave and then slowly walked back down the hill to do their chores. The last two men finished covering Johnny's coffin while Sam and Casey stood by, watching and keeping vigilant.

It was a solemn time for all of Willard's men. Everyone had liked Johnny and everyone had worked with him at one time or another. They were going to miss him.

As Sam stood looking at the grave, he was wondering if this was just the beginning of what was to come. He couldn't help but think Johnny would probably be only the first of many who would die a senseless death if things didn't change soon. It angered him to think greed could make it so easy for one man to kill another.

When they were finished covering Johnny and everyone had gone, Sam and Casey stood at the freshly covered grave looking down at it. Each was filled with his own thoughts.

"I better get to work," Casey said softly.

"Yeah," Sam replied with a sigh, then turned and started back toward the ranch house with Casey.

"Casey, get a couple of hands together and saddle my horse. We're going out to where Johnny was found. I want to take a look around."

"Yes, sir."

When they got to the yard, Sam went on to the house while Casey went to the barn. In a short time, Casey had rounded up two of the men who had found Johnny. The three of them saddled their horses as well as Sam's big black stallion. They walked the horses across the yard to the front of the ranch house, Casey leading Sam's horse and a horse for himself.

When Sam came out of the house, he still had a six-gun strapped on his hip, but now he was carrying his Winchester rifle as well. Sam reached up and took the reins to his horse from Casey and stepped up alongside the horse. He slid his rifle into the scabbard, put his foot into the stirrup and swung his leg over the saddle. Seated in the saddle, he looked at his men.

"You ready?"

"We're ready, boss," Casey answered.

"Okay, take me to where you found Johnny."

Sam noticed each of them had a rifle on their saddle and a handgun in their holster. They were ready for trouble and ready to fight. He only hoped the guns would not be necessary.

The two ranch hands Casey had picked out were Slim White, a long time hand at the ranch; and Bill Smith, a fairly new hand.

Slim was a tall and lean man with a little gray in his long handlebar mustache. His eyes were dark gray and saw everything. He had a good many scars on his face from when he was in the Army during the Civil War. Like many men, he had come west after the war to start a new life.

Bill Smith had been too young to be in the war, but he was a capable young man. He was not very tall, but he was stocky and able to take care of himself. His long blond hair stuck out from under his hat and his blue eyes sparkled with a certain devilment.

They pulled back on the reins of their horses as they backed away from the hitching rail and turned toward the barn. Slim and Bill kicked their horses in the side with their spurs and started galloping out of the yard and onto the pasture behind the barn. Casey and Sam followed along behind them.

The two riders set an easy pace for the horses. They were good men. They knew how to get the most out of their horses without being too hard on them. As the four of them rode out across the prairie they all kept an eye out for danger, as it was a dangerous time.

The cattle were spread out in an effort to find enough grass to eat. Sam could not remember when he had seen the grass so brown and the watering holes as low on water as they were now.

After riding for some time, the four riders came to the top of a knoll. The two lead riders pulled back on their reins and stopped. Sam and Casey rode up beside them and looked out over the open space.

"We found Johnny down there," Bill said as he pointed toward the watering hole at the bottom of the hill.

"Yeah, he was laying face down close to the water," Slim added.

Sam sat in the saddle and looked down at the watering hole before he started looking around. There were very few trees on this part of the ranch, but Sam could see there was a small cluster of trees about fifty yards or so off to the south and west of the watering hole along a dry shallow draw. He looked first at the trees and then at the watering hole. After studying the lay of the land, the location of the trees in relation to the watering hole, and the watering hole, he looked over at Slim.

"Tell me, was Johnny lying with his back toward those trees?" Sam asked, directing his question to Slim.

Slim looked off toward the trees then toward the watering hole. He seemed to be studying the area, nodding his head slightly as he did.

"Yeah, I think so," Slim replied.

Sam looked over at Bill as if he expected Bill to answer the same question.

"Yeah, he was," Bill replied.

"My guess is whoever shot him was lying in wait in those trees."

"That makes sense," Casey agreed.

"Where was Johnny's horse?"

"He was over there," Slim said as he pointed toward the other side of the watering hole. "We figured he run off a little ways. The shots probably scared him a little."

"I'm sure you're right. Let's go down there, but keep your eyes open. My guess would be Johnny was bushwhacked from the trees."

Sam nudged his horse forward. He moved slowly and carefully down the hill toward the watering hole with the others close behind. As they moved closer to the watering hole and closer to the grove of trees, the four men spread out to make it harder to be taken by surprise. Sam was keeping an eye on the small grove of trees. He figured if trouble were going to come to them, it would come from there.

Sam and Casey moved closer and closer to the trees. As they approached them, Sam reached down and drew his rifle from the scabbard and levered a cartridge into the chamber. The others saw what he had done and did the same.

When Sam got close to the edge of the trees, he stopped and looked around. Every nerve in his body was tense and telling him to be careful.

Sam stepped out of the saddle, but never took his eyes off the trees. He dropped the reins to his horse on the ground and quickly glanced at the others. Gripping his rifle in both hands, he took a step or two closer to the trees.

Suddenly, Sam heard the sound of movement in the brush back in the small grove. He jerked his rifle to his shoulder as he readied himself for a fight, but there was silence. He again glanced at the others over his shoulder. They were all sitting atop their horses with their rifles at the ready. Ready to take on whoever might have the nerve to challenge them.

"Casey, cover me," Sam said without turning his head to look back at Casey.

Casey stepped down from the saddle and moved quickly up next to Sam. Casey knelt down and put his rifle to his shoulder. He then nodded at Sam to let him know he was ready.

Sam stepped into the grove and leaned up against one of the trees. As he looked down to make sure he didn't step on something that might cause him to loose his balance, he saw something shinny on the ground. He took a quick look at Casey. Seeing that Casey was in a position to cover him, he bent down and picked it up.

Suddenly there was the rustle of bushes in among the trees. Everyone jumped and took aim in the direction the sound had come from. They were all able to breathe a sigh of relief when a large mule deer jumped out of the grove and bounded off across the prairie.

Sam turned and looked at Casey as he let out a sigh of relief. He smiled and shook his head. At least this time it was nothing, but next time it might be different.

Sam moved away from the trees holding his rifle loosely in his hand. He knew there would not be anyone in the grove if the deer had been there.

CHAPTER NINE

As Sam walked toward Casey, he examined the 40-60 caliber metal casing he found at the edge of the grove. There were two thoughts that came to mind as he looked at it. The first thing Sam thought about was why was the shooter leaving the cartridge casings lying around? Was it possible they were being left because the shooter was in a hurry to get away? Although it was a possible reason, it didn't seem to be likely in this case. There had been no one around to cause the shooter to want to get out of there in a hurry. Johnny had been checking the water holes alone. As far as Sam knew there had been no one else in the area. The shooter would have had all the time in the world to pick up the casing and still get away without being seen.

Was it possible whoever was doing the shooting left them there to serve some propose? That seemed to be the better question as Sam had only found one casing and Johnny had been shot twice in the back.

The second thing Sam thought about was why did the shooter pick Johnny as his target? He was just a ranch hand checking the watering holes. Johnny had no enemies Sam knew of, and he was no threat to anyone. Was it possible that it didn't matter who had been checking the watering holes?

If that was the case, the shooter had to be doing it to let Sam know his men were easy targets.

"What did yah find, boss?" Casey asked interrupting Sam's thoughts.

"This," he replied as he held out the shiny brass cartridge casing.

Casey took the cartridge and examined it.

"That's from a 40-60 caliber rifle. The same as we found the other day by the looks of it. I'd guess it's from the same gun," Casey said looking up at Sam.

It was easy to see the puzzled look on Casey's face. It was obvious he had some of the same questions Sam had.

"Yeah. I find it interesting that a shooter would leave them behind. These are not a very common cartridge around here. It's almost like leaving a signature," Sam said thoughtfully as he started walking toward the watering hole.

Casey looked from the cartridge casing to Sam. He wondered what was going through Sam's mind. Casey followed along behind Sam as he walked to the place where Johnny's body had been found. When Casey caught up to Sam, he was kneeling on the ground and looking around.

"What yah lookin' for?" Casey asked.

"I think Johnny was kneeling right about here when he was shot in the back. He had gotten off his horse for some reason and was kneeling down in the dirt near the watering hole."

Sam turned and looked back over his shoulder toward the small grove of trees. He glanced up to see if Bill and Slim were still sitting in their saddles and keeping watch while Sam and Casey looked around. Sam quickly realized it would be a fairly easy shot from the trees to where Johnny had fallen. Anyone with a saddle rifle could have killed Johnny. Even someone who was just a fair shot with a pistol could have killed him from there. Sam could see no reason for the use of such a long-range rifle.

"Whoever shot Johnny knew I sent riders out everyday to make the rounds of the watering holes," Sam said.

"That's no big secret, boss. Most ranchers do that at times like these," Casey said, not sure what Sam was talking about.

"That's true, but why was Johnny off his horse? He didn't need to get out of the saddle to see how much water was in the hole."

"Beats me. You suppose he saw somethin'," Casey asked.

"Yes I do. I think what he saw was right here," Sam said as he pointed at the ground. "If you look here in the dirt, you can see there was a small box or something square set down here. If you look closely you can see where the corners of the box were. See it?"

"Yeah. I see it," Casey replied as he looked at the ground where Sam was pointing.

"I'd be willing to bet someone put a box, or something shaped like one, there in the dirt to get the attention of anyone who came to check the watering hole. Johnny must have seen it and got down from his horse to check it out. While he was off his horse, he was bushwhacked from the grove of trees," Sam said as he put together a mental picture of what he thought happened.

"You think it was some sort of trick to get Johnny off his horse and bent down so he couldn't defend his self?"

"That's a good possibility, Casey. It looks to me like our shooter was being very careful not to get himself shot. It's fairly common knowledge that Johnny was real good with a handgun. Shooting him in the back would be the only way to be sure he couldn't shoot back. At this range, if Johnny had been able to shoot back, the shooter would have risked his own life."

"So yah think they was out to get Johnny?"

Sam looked around for a bit before he answered Casey. He mulled over in his mind what he had been thinking earlier.

"No. I don't think so. I don't think whoever shot Johnny cared who was checking the watering holes. I think they were more interested in sending me a message."

Casey just looked at Sam for a moment, then stood up. He glanced over at the other two riders standing guard. Sam's comment had confused him. He wasn't sure what Sam was trying to tell him.

"What kind of message?" Casey asked as he turned back to look at Sam.

"The kind of message that says they will do anything to get control of this ranch and the water on it," Sam replied.

"It's kind of hard to think we got neighbors thinkin' that away," Casey said shaking his head in disbelief.

"Yes, it is. What's really got me stumped is the 40-60 caliber casings."

"I don't understand," Casey said, again looking confused.

"Have you noticed they show up at each sight where a shooting has taken place?"

"Yeah. I noticed that."

"Yet, no one around here has a 40-60 caliber rifle, at least that we know of."

"What yah getting at, boss?"

"When you start adding things up, it looks like whoever is after my ranch has hired himself someone from outside the area to help."

"I see," Casey said as he thought about what Sam had said. "The two gunmen in town, the one that shot at yah at the ranch house and the one that shot Johnny, all adds up to hired gunmen to me."

114

"One thing we know for sure is the one who shot Johnny is not one of those who were in town shooting at me. That means we have at least one other gunman, maybe more," Sam said as he thought about what he needed to do about it.

"I agree. But ain't it a little dumb to go around leavin' those brass casing where we can find 'um? They ain't very common around these parts," Casey asked.

"That depends."

"Depends on what?" Casey asked, not sure what Sam was thinking now.

"On what kind of a message they want to send me."

"I don't get it," Casey said, the expression on his face and the sound of his voice showing how baffled he was by what was happening.

"I'm beginning to think the bullet missed me at the ranch house on propose. I think the shooter intended to miss me. I think he wanted me to know he could get me anytime and anyplace he wanted, including on my own front porch."

"What about Johnny? Killin' him don't get them no wheres."

"It might. I think the shooter wanted to let me know he could pick off any one of my hands and there is nothing I can do about it. Whoever it is, he's a good shot with that rifle."

"You mean like one of them sharpshooter fellas durin' the war?" Casey asked.

Sam looked at Casey. Casey had hit the nail on the head.

"That's exactly what I mean, Casey," Sam said with a hint of excitement in his voice. "I wouldn't be surprised if our shooter had been a sharpshooter during the Great War."

"Well, to my way of thinkin' that don't narrow it down none too much. We've got a lot of neighbors that was in the war. Heck, we've even got a couple of Rebs working here," Casey said.

"You're right about that. We have some from both sides of the war," Sam agreed.

Suddenly, dirt jumped up from the ground as a bullet hit only inches from Sam's feet followed by the loud crack of rifle fire. Both Sam and Casey dove to the ground. Before Sam could turn around to see what was happening, he could hear the sound of rifle fire coming from near him. He looked up and saw his men returning fire to where the shot had come from.

Sam quickly looked in the direction his men were shooting, but he could not see anything. The prairie was void of any life all the way to the top of a knoll several hundred yards away. The only place the shot could have come from was the top of the knoll. Whoever had taken the shot at him was probably long gone down the other side by now.

Way too far away for anyone to see who it was, or to be able to catch him.

"Hold your fire. Hold your fire," Sam called out.

The men stopped shooting and looked toward Sam. Sam was getting to his feet.

"You want us to go after him, boss?" Bill asked, his voice showing how excited he was.

"No. You'd never catch him. He's got too much of a head start on you," Sam said as he brushed the dirt off his pants. "Did you get a chance to see who it was?"

"No," Slim replied. "I just saw someone disappear over the top of the hill. Didn't get a good 'nough look to tell who it was. Sorry, boss."

"Get the boss's horse," Casey ordered as he got up off the ground.

While Slim rode off to retrieve Sam's horse, Casey stood next to Sam.

"I'd be willin' to bet we'll find another 40-60 caliber casing on top of that hill," Casey said.

"You'd probably be right," Sam agreed.

Slim returned with Sam's horse. Taking hold of the reins, Sam put his foot in the stirrup and swung up into the saddle. He sat in the saddle as he waited for Casey to walk over and get his horse. As soon as they were all mounted, he swung his horse around and started up the knoll at a trot. Casey and the other ranch hands followed close behind, all of them ready in case the shooting wasn't over.

Sam stopped on top of the knoll and looked out over the prairie. There was no one in sight. He nudged his horse over toward where he thought the shot had come from and began looking around on the ground for some sign of where the shooter had been. It didn't take him long to find where the sharpshooter had laid down on the ground to take his shot at him. It was no surprise when he saw another 40-60 caliber casing lying on the ground in plain view.

Sam took a quick look around, then stepped down off his horse and looked at the marks left in the ground by the sharpshooter. He could see where the shooter's elbows had left little indentations in the dry dirt. He could also see where the toes of the shooter's boots had been while he laid down on his stomach to take his shot.

Sam saw another set of markings in the ground. There were two small holes about an inch deep in the dirt and about a foot apart, a little less than three feet forward of the marks left by the shooter's elbows. He wasn't sure what would have made the two holes.

"Casey, come over here."

Casey climbed down off his horse and walked over next to Sam.

"What do you make of these?" Sam asked as he knelt down and pointed at the two evenly spaced holes.

Casey knelt down and looked at all the marks on the ground. He studied the markings and looked at the area around them. He couldn't come up with any idea as to what might have caused the two holes.

"No idea, boss," Casey said as he looked at Sam and shook his head.

"Casey, lie down on the ground next to those markings and hold your rifle out as if you were going take a shot at someone down at the watering hole."

Casey was a little puzzled by his boss's request, but he laid down along side the other marks in the dirt. As soon as he was in position and had a chance to look down the hill toward the watering hole, he turned his head and looked up at Sam.

"That's a long shot from here, boss," Casey said.

"Yes, it is," Sam agreed.

"I don't think many men could hit anythin' down there from here," Casey commented as he looked down the hill toward the watering hole.

"Maybe not, but if you had some kind of a support on the end of your rifle it would make it a lot easier, wouldn't it?"

"It sure would, but it's still a tough shot," Casey replied as he suddenly began to understand what his boss was getting at.

"From the looks of the marks left on the ground, our sharpshooter was a little shorter than you are, Casey. You're what, about five feet ten, aren't you?

"I'm five nine," Casey said nodding his head.

That would make our shooter about five feet five inches tall, maybe a little less. He also had some sort of support on the front of his rifle to steady it."

Casey got up off the ground and brushed the dirt off his clothes as he listened to Sam. He was beginning to understand what they were up against.

"Our man is fairly short and has a great deal of experience as a sharpshooter. That means we're dealing with someone who doesn't like to get close to his work, but he is good at it."

"That doesn't put us any closer to finding out who it is," Casey said.

"Maybe, maybe not," Sam replied thoughtfully as he turned and walked back to his horse.

Casey was not sure what his boss had on his mind, but it was clear he was thinking about something. Casey thought about asking, but figured his boss would tell him when he got around to it.

Sam swung into the saddle and waited for Casey to mount up. As soon as Casey was mounted, he turned his horse back toward the ranch house. The four men rode across the prairie at a pretty good gallop toward the ranch house.

CHAPTER TEN

As Sam rode into the ranch yard with his men, he saw a Palomino horse tied to the hitching rail in front of the ranch house. Palominos were rare in this part of the country. Sam could not remember ever having seen that horse in the valley before. He was curious as to who the horse might belong to.

Sam also saw one of his ranch hands standing on the porch next to the door. He took a look around to see if there were still guards at the barn and haystacks. They were still there. Sam could see nothing to indicate there was anything wrong. He had to wonder why one of the ranch hands was standing guard on the front porch.

"You recognize the horse?" Sam asked to Casey as they rode toward the ranch house.

"No. Ain't never seen that one 'fore. It's a real nice lookin' horse, though. Yah don't see horses like that around these parts much."

"No, you don't. I think we better find out who has come to pay us a visit."

Casey just nodded and rode along side Sam to the house while Slim and Bill went to the barn to put up their horses. When Sam and Casey got to the house, they swung down out of their saddles and tied their horses to the hitching rail. Sam reached out and gently patted the Palomino on the neck. He gave the horse a good looking over before stepping up on the porch.

"What's going on?" Sam asked the ranch hand on the porch.

"There's a lady come all the way out here to see you, sir. She's a mighty fine lookin' woman, too," the ranch hand said with a smile.

"Who is she?"

The ranch hand shrugged his shoulders indicating he didn't know the woman's name. Sam looked at Casey as he wondered what was going on. It was obvious that the only way he was going to find out was to go inside and meet her.

"Put our horses up, please," Sam instructed the ranch hand.

"Yes sir," he replied, then stepped off the porch, untied the two horses and led them off across the yard toward the barn.

Casey followed Sam into the ranch house. Once inside, they saw a young woman sitting on the sofa sipping coffee. Margaret was sitting in one of the chairs near the woman. She had apparently been keeping his guest company until he returned.

Sam looked at his guest. The young woman had long blond hair and sky blue eyes. The sun had nicely tanned the smooth skin of her face. The woman set the cup of coffee down on the table and stood up. She looked Sam over and smiled.

Sam noticed the woman was wearing jeans that clung nicely to her curved hips, and a red plaid shirt that did little to hide the fact there was a woman under it. There was no doubt in Sam's mind that she filled out the jeans and shirt rather well. Although, it was not the first time he had seen a woman in what were most commonly considered men's clothes, it was the first time he had seen a woman wear them so well.

"Mr. Willard, this is Miss Helen Westerman," Margaret said introducing his guest.

"Nice to meet you, Miss Westerman. This is Casey, my foreman."

She nodded toward Casey and then turned back to Sam.

"Good morning, sir," she said with a pleasant tone in her voice. "I'm sure you are wondering why I'm here."

"As a matter of fact, yes I am," Sam replied.

"The reason I am here is that I have heard you have a young man working for you by the name of John Westerman. Is that correct?" she asked, her eyes filled with hope.

Sam looked at Casey, then back at the woman before he replied. "I'm sorry, but you have come a long ways for nothing. I don't have any John Westerman working for me."

Sam motioned for her to sit back down.

"Are you sure that he is supposed to be working for me."

"That is what I was told," she said, the look on her face showing her disappointment.

"I'm sorry, but you were apparently misinformed. I have no one by that name here."

"I visited with your local barkeeper at the Red Garter Saloon in Shallow Creek. Jake, I believe was his name. From the description I gave him, he believes you might know him as Johnny Marsh."

The mention of Johnny Marsh caught both Sam and Casey off guard. How was he going to tell this woman they had buried Johnny Marsh that very morning? In fact, they had just returned from where he had been killed. No one on the ranch had known him by the name of Westerman, at least as far as Sam knew.

"What is wrong?" the woman asked, a little confused by the expression on Sam's face.

"I'm not sure how to tell you this, but I'm sorry to inform you that Johnny Marsh, or John Westerman, was laid to rest early this morning," Sam explained as gently as he knew how.

The woman looked at Sam for a few seconds, then her face turned pale and her mouth fell open. Her eyes got big as she looked at Sam in disbelief. It was a shock for her to have come all this way to see her brother only to find out he had just been buried.

"Are you all right?" Sam asked.

"Yes," she said softly as she slowly tipped her head down.

It was clear to Casey and Sam that this had come as a shock to her, but then why wouldn't it? There was no way for her to know Johnny had been killed. He hadn't even had time to tell the sheriff, not that telling the sheriff would make any difference.

Sam and Casey knew it was not uncommon for a ranch hand to give a false name when he was hired to work cattle. Some didn't want to be found for one reason or another, while others were trying to leave their past behind and start a new life for themselves. Johnny had worked hard and had proven himself to be a good ranch hand. That was far more important than his past or his real name.

After a long period of silence, Helen Westerman slowly looked up at Sam. Her eyes were filled with tears and they began rolling down her cheeks.

"Where is he now?" she asked in a soft voice.

"We buried him up on the hill under a big cottonwood tree this morning," Sam explained.

"It's a real nice spot," Casey added, hoping it might help ease some of the pain for her.

"I'm sure it is. I would like to see his grave, if I may. Will you take me there, please?" her voice almost pleading with him to grant her request.

"Certainly," Sam replied.

Sam turned to Casey and said, "Get a couple of the hands and my horse.

Casey didn't reply. He simply turned and left the room.

Helen watched as Casey left the house. She wondered why Sam wanted "a couple of the hands". All she wanted to do was see where Johnny had been buried.

"Are you sure Johnny Marsh is the man you are looking for?" Sam asked.

"Yes. Well, I believe he is," she replied, not really sure.

"Then you aren't certain?"

"Well, I guess not," she replied after giving it a moment's thought. "Would you be so kind as to describe him to me?"

"Better yet, why don't you describe him to me," Sam suggested.

"Well, he is about five foot ten inches tall. He has light sandy brown hair and deep brown eyes. He looks a lot like his dad, but then you wouldn't know that. He is rather slim, but very strong. Oh, he has a small scar on his left cheek just below his eye," she explained.

Everything she told him fit Johnny Marsh to a T. But Sam also knew those were all things anyone could see if they took the time to look at him. The only thing he could remember that not everyone would know about was how Johnny had gotten the scar on his cheek. Sam could remember Johnny telling him and hoped he hadn't told anyone else.

"I don't mean to be, well, suspicious, but would you mind telling me how Johnny got that scare?"

"I understand," she said politely. "I'm rather embarrassed to admit it, but I gave it to him."

"How did it happen?" Sam asked.

"When John and I were just kids, we were at a family picnic back in Ohio. We were playing horseshoes. Just as I was swinging the horseshoe back to throw it, John stepped behind me and I hit him in the face with the horseshoe. It cut him pretty bad, but it healed up well. You could hardly see the scar when he got older."

"Then Johnny was your brother?"

"Yes," she replied softly.

Just as Sam was about to ask her more about her brother, Casey came in the door.

"We're ready, boss."

"Be right with you, Casey."

Helen looked toward the door where Casey was standing. She could see two well-armed men sitting astride their horses in front of the house. They were waiting for them.

"Excuse me, but would you mind explaining why we need an armed escort to go where my brother is buried?"

"I don't mean to alarm you, but we've been having a little difficulty around here. This whole valley is a tinder box and is likely to go up in flames at any time."

"I don't understand," she said as she looked at Sam for an explanation.

"Your brother was killed while he was checking watering holes on this ranch. The drought has made some people around here angry and jealous of those of us they think have more water than they do."

"You mean John was shot over water?" she said with surprise.

Sam could not but notice her surprise. If she didn't understand the importance of water on a ranch like this, she must have led a protected life, he thought.

"Water is the life blood out here. Without it, ranching is impossible. We don't have a lot of rain here like you do back in Ohio. There have been range wars fought over it, and there may very well be another one right here if we don't get some rain pretty soon."

"Oh, I see. You are right though, we do have more water back in Ohio. I did notice it looked terribly dry here," she replied as she began to understand.

"It is dry," Sam said as he stood up. "Would you like to go visit your brother's grave now?"

"Yes, of course," she replied.

Helen stood up and walked to the door. As Sam held the door for her, she stepped out onto the porch. The men sitting astride their horses watched her as she walked over to her horse and untied it. She put her foot in the stirrup and gracefully swung her leg over the saddle, sitting down in the saddle in one smooth motion.

Sam took the reins of his black horse from one of the ranch hands, put his foot in the stirrup and swung into the saddle. As soon as he was ready, he looked around to make sure everyone else was ready before he turned his horse away from the hitching rail and started off across the yard.

Helen nudged her horse up along side Sam. As they started off across the prairie, Helen glanced back over her shoulder at the men following along behind. The two men who had been assigned to escort them had their rifles held in their hands and laid across their laps. They were continually looking around. It gave Helen an uneasy feeling.

"How far is it to where my brother is buried?" she asked.

"Not far. Just over there by that tree," he replied as he pointed off toward an old cottonwood on the top of a hill.

"Do you really think it is necessary to have an armed escort this close to the ranch house?"

"Yes. Yes I do. No one on this ranch is to travel alone, and no one is to go anywhere outside the bunk house unarmed."

"I wouldn't think it would be necessary so close to the ranch house."

"Let me assure you that it is. Just the other day I was shot at while I was standing on my front porch."

Helen looked at him. She knew she had come out to the Wild West, but she had not expected it to be this wild. It was becoming clear to her that this was still a dangerous country.

As they rode up the hill, Helen didn't say anything more. She seemed to be wrapped up in her own thoughts. Sam was not sure if she was thinking about her brother and who might have killed him, or if she was thinking about what he had said about it being dangerous to travel alone. Either way, she was getting the message that this wide-open country was not safe.

As they approached the fresh grave where Johnny had been laid to rest, Sam motioned for the two riders to spread out and keep their eyes open while Helen visited her brother's grave. He swung out of his saddle, then watched as Helen got down off her horse. He reached out and she handed him the reins. Sam walked off a little ways with the horses in order to give Helen a few moments alone with her brother. It was the least he could do for her.

CHAPTER ELEVEN

Sam watched Helen as she walked closer to her brother's grave. He didn't want to disturb her in her moment of grief so he stepped back out of the way. He found it was almost impossible to take his eyes off her as she walked with such smooth graceful movements. Her long blond hair waved in the gentle breeze as she moved toward the grave.

He couldn't help but notice how nicely she filled out the snug fitting jeans. Her hips swayed gently as she moved. The flare of her hips from her narrow waist helped to form the smooth flowing lines of her body. There was no doubt in Sam's mind that Helen was a beautiful woman.

As she knelt down beside Johnny's grave, Sam turned and looked away. Looking at her the way he was seemed inappropriate under the circumstances. She was saying something, maybe a prayer, or maybe she was just telling him something she wanted him to know. Either way, Sam could not hear her. Sam didn't really want to hear what she had to say to her brother. He felt these few moments should be private, just between her and her brother.

As soon as Helen stood up, Sam turned and walked their horses closer to her. He saw tears in her eyes. He wanted to say something that would make everything all right, but there was nothing he could say that would do that. Instead, he simply held out the reins to her horse and waited for her to take them from him.

Just as she was about to take hold of the reins, a bullet struck the tree only a few feet away and a shot rang out. It scattered little pieces of the bark into the air.

Sam dropped the reins to the horses and grabbed Helen by the arm. He jerked her up against him, then dove to the ground at the base of the old cottonwood tree, taking her with him. He quickly tucked her close to him and rolled up over her. Sam drew his gun as he covered her with his body in an attempt to protect her.

Instantly, the air was filled with the sounds of gunfire. The two men who had escorted them to the grave site were shooting at a lone rider who was making tracks off in the distance. It wasn't long and all the shooting had stopped.

"All clear, boss," one of the riders said.

Sam looked down at Helen. She was looking up at him. He rolled off of her and stood up. He reached down to help Helen to her feet, but she laid on the ground looking up at him. It was almost as if she was in shock.

"Are you all right?" Sam asked, afraid he may have hurt her.

"Yes," she replied as she let out a long sigh. "I'm okay, I think."

"I'm sorry if I hurt you. I didn't mean to be so rough. Please, let me help you up," Sam said as he reached out again to her.

Helen slowly reached up and took hold of Sam's hands. She never took her eyes off Sam's face as he gently, but firmly pulled her to her feet. She felt a little weak in the knees and short of breath. To steady herself, she reached up and put her hands on Sam's broad shoulders. This was a first for her. She had never had anyone shoot at her before.

Sam wasn't sure what he should do, but he did not want her to fall. He slipped his arms around her and drew her close to him. She was breathing rapidly and looked a little flushed. He could feel her body tremble as she leaned against him for support.

Helen looked up at Sam's face for a moment. She slipped her arms around his neck as she laid her head on his shoulder and closed her eyes. Helen slowly began to regain her composure from the shooting. She also began to realize she liked being in his arms. She could feel his strength as he held her to him. The feel of her body pressing tightly against his strong chest gave her a secure feeling, something she had not felt in a very long time. This tall stranger, though roughly, had protected her from harm.

Now her mind was beginning to turn to other thoughts. Thoughts she should not be having with a man that she had only known for barely an hour. It was those thoughts that began to frighten her more than the shooting had.

She took her arms from around his neck and slid her hands down onto his broad chest. Slowly, almost reluctantly, she pushed herself back as she looked up at him.

"I'm sorry. I'm not used to getting shot at," she said as a way of apologizing for her behavior as well as her thoughts.

"I'm sure that's true," Sam said as he halfheartedly took his hands off her narrow waist and allowed her to straighten up.

Sam took hold of her arm when she still appeared to be a little unstable. He simply stood there waiting to make sure she could stand without help. Sam let go of her and watched her as she backed away from him and looked off across the prairie.

Helen wasn't sure if she could stand without help as she backed away from him. Still feeling a little unsteady, she looked out over the prairie then turned her back to him. The feel of his arms around her had done as much, if not more, to unsettle her nerves as the shooting. She took a couple of deep breaths as she tried to regain her composure. When she felt she could face him again, she turned back around.

"I want to thank you for protecting me," she said as she looked up at him, her voice still a little shaky.

"I'm sorry if I was a little rough with you."

Helen did not reply. She was still feeling flushed, even a little embarrassed. She had found Sam to be tall and handsome, as well as somewhat seductive. She was no longer sure if the feelings running through her were the result of the shooting, or from the feeling of being so close to him. Either way, it was rather disquieting for her.

"I'm sorry this had to happen to you, but I think I can assure you the bullet was most likely not meant to hit you. I'm sure that doesn't make it any easier to take. The shot was most likely meant to scare you."

Helen looked at him for a minute before she replied. "You are right. Whether the bullet was meant for me or not does very little to make me feel better, but it does make very clear what you told me earlier about the possibility of a range war."

"Say, boss?" Bill called out interrupting Sam.

"Yeah?" Sam asked as he turned to look at him.

"That wasn't the same guy that fired on us earlier."

"Are you sure?"

"Yeah. That wasn't any 40-60 caliber rifle shot. That was from a 30-30, probably a Winchester. And whoever it was this time, he was a lot closer."

Sam had not had time to see where the shot had come from. He had been too busy doing what he could to protect Helen. He looked over toward where Bill was pointing.

Bill was right. It had not been the "sharpshooter" this time, or at least if it was he had used a different rifle. However, that didn't seem likely to Sam. It was probably a different shooter. Sam knew that shooters tend to favor one type of gun they are good with and don't often change.

"Did you get a look at who it was?"

"Not a good look, but I think I've seen that horse somewhere before. I just can't place it."

"Around here?"

"Yeah, I think so," Bill said, thoughtfully.

"Keep trying to remember where you saw it. If you remember, you let me know."

"Will do, boss."

"We better get Miss Westerman back to the ranch house. I'm sure she will feel a lot safer there."

Sam walked over to Helen's horse. He gave her a hand as she put her foot in the stirrup and swung her leg over the saddle. Sam then swung into the saddle on his horse and motioned the others to start back toward the ranch house. Sam was not about to send his ranch hands after the shooter. His first priority was to protect Helen.

As they rode down the hill, Sam and the others kept a watch out for anyone who might be around that didn't belong there. They had seen the shooter ride off, but they were not sure where he might have gone. It was possible he might try to circle around and ambush them somewhere else as they were going back to the ranch house.

Sam kept thinking about what his ranch hand had said about having seen the shooter's horse. He had not gotten a good look at the horse himself as he was on the ground trying to protect Helen from harm. If one of his ranch hands had seen the horse before, then there was a good chance it was from around here. His ranch hands didn't get too far from the ranch very often. A trip into town once a month was about it. They rarely left the valley, if ever.

Once back at the ranch house, Sam escorted Helen into the house. They were met by Margaret.

"Would you show Miss Westerman to the guest room? She might want to freshen up a bit before lunch."

"Certainly. I heard some shooting. Is everyone okay?" Margaret asked.

"Yes. A little shaken up, but okay," he said, then turned toward Helen.

"Please feel free to make yourself at home. I have a few things to take care of, then I'll be back."

"Mr. Willard?"

"Please, call me, Sam," he replied as he looked at her and waited for her to ask her question.

Helen wasn't sure she should call him, Sam. The use of first names seemed to put them on more intimate terms. She was not sure she should do anything that might make her feel closer to him, but it didn't seem right not to call him by his first name after what he had done for her.

"All right, Sam," she replied with a slight smile. "I need to know. Was Johnny a good ranch hand?"

"Yes, he was. He was a very good ranch hand and everyone here liked him."

"Thank you," she said, then she turned toward Margaret.

Sam watched her as she followed Margaret out of the living room. He turned and went outside.

After stepping out on the front porch, Sam stopped and looked around as if he was looking for someone. He saw a well armed ranch hand standing guard next to the corral by the barn. He was keeping watch out across the open land. There was also a ranch hand near the bunkhouse keeping watch in the other direction.

Sam looked toward the barn. He knew Casey had taken the horses to the barn to unsaddle and wipe them down. He stepped off the porch and walked across the yard toward the barn.

When he stepped through the open door of the barn, he saw Casey wiping down Helen's Palomino. Bill had already finished wiping down Sam's horse and was leading the black stallion into a stall.

"Casey, as soon as you have had lunch, I want you to take three or four men with you and go take a look around the place where the last shooter shot at us."

"Okay. Yah lookin' for anythin' special?"

"Yeah, tracks. I want to know where the shooter came from and where he went."

"How far do you want us to trail him?"

"Just to the edge of the ranch. I don't want you to leave the ranch, you understand?"

"Yes, sir," Casey replied.

"If you lose his tracks, return here. I don't want you to get into any kind of a gunfight. If you run into trouble, come straight back. And I want you back by dark even if you have to leave a good trail. I don't want any of you taking any chances."

"Got yah," Casey said.

"I'll take care of Miss Westerman's horse. I want you to gather up who you're going to take with you and go get something to eat. You can leave as soon as you've finished eating."

Casey nodded his head to indicate he understood and handed the rag to Sam. Sam finished rubbing down Helen's horse, then led it into a stall next to his stallion. After filling the trough with feed and making sure the horse had been well taken care of, he returned to the house.

On his way to the house, Sam again took a look around. The ranch hands standing watch waved at him to let him know that all was well. He couldn't help but think all was not well. There was no doubt in his mind it wasn't likely to get any better without some badly needed rain. One look at the sky made it perfectly clear there would not be any rain today.

As Sam stepped into the house, he found Helen sitting on the sofa in the living room. He was surprised to see her there as he had had Margaret show her to the guest room. She was looking a little depressed to say the least, but that seemed natural enough considering what she had gone through this day.

"Lunch will be ready pretty soon," Sam said.

"I don't know if I can eat," she said as she looked up at him with sad eyes.

"Well, you need to eat something," Sam said as he sat down in a chair near her.

"I want to thank you for all your help today. And I especially want to thank you for taking care of Johnny."

"You're welcome. I'm sure it has been a rough day for you. If you would like, you are welcome to stay here until you feel more like traveling. Margaret will be happy to keep a plate warm for you if you wish to rest for awhile."

140

"Thank you. That's very nice of you. I think I will take you up on your kind offer," she said with a soft smile.

"Great. I'll let Margaret know you will be staying with us awhile longer," Sam said as he stood up.

Sam left the living room and headed out to the kitchen. Margaret was busy making sure the ranch hands were getting enough to eat.

"Miss Westerman told me you saved her life," Margaret said as she poured more gravy into a bowl to set on the table.

"I don't think the shooter was shooting at her."

"He may not have been shooting at her, but she feels you protected her just the same."

Her comment made Sam feel a little embarrassed. He had done what he thought was the right thing to do at the time. It was done more from instinct than from something he had taken time to think about.

"I would like you to keep a plate warm for Miss Westerman. She is feeling a little tired and would like to lie down for a while. She isn't ready to leave just yet."

"Certainly, Mr. Willard."

Sam watched as Margaret wiped her hands on her apron, picked up a bowl of potatoes and left the kitchen for the dinning hall. As soon as she left, Sam picked up a plate and filled it with food. He then sat down with the ranch hands that had come in for lunch.

The first thing he noticed was there were fewer men at the table than usual. It was easy to understand as some of the men were out checking watering holes and cattle while some were standing guard around the ranch house. Those ranch hands would come in to eat when the others relieved them.

Sam watched as four men finished eating and got up. Casey got up with them.

"I'll see you later," Casey said as he set his dirty dishes next to the water pump for Margaret to take care of.

"Casey, take a good look at any tracks you find. We just might be able to figure out who is doing the shooting."

"Right," Casey replied.

"You be careful out there," Sam reminded Casey. "I don't want to bury anyone else."

"Will do. I don't want to be the next one yah bury," Casey replied then turned and left the kitchen.

Sam watched as the men left. Casey had been a long time foreman for Sam. He had also been a long time friend. Sam knew the place could run without Casey, but it wouldn't be the same and it wouldn't run as smoothly without him. Sam began to realize how much he depended on Casey and how much he would miss him if something should happen to him.

CHAPTER TWELVE

Sam spent the better part of the afternoon at his desk in the corner of the living room going over his books. He knew this year was going to be tough, but he had been through tough times before. This year he would do well to meet the operating expenses and wages for his ranch hands if it did not rain soon. Although it would be tough, he had no doubt he would survive the drought. He also knew some of the ranchers in the valley would not survive if the drought continued much longer.

As Sam sat back and looked at the papers on his desk, his thoughts turned to the men that he had sent out to follow the tracks of the latest shooter. His men never seemed to complain, and seemed to be as loyal as any employer could want. All his men were hard workers and followed orders well. Some of them had been with him for years, while others were fairly new to his ranch.

Casey was a top rate foreman with nothing but the ranch as his prime interest. He worked along side the men, earning a day's wages for a day's work as well as the respect of the other ranch hands.

Even with that thought in mind, Sam was well aware his ranch hands had not been hired for their ability to use a gun. Even though several of them were rather good with a gun and they were all ready to use a gun when necessary, none of them were what would be considered gunfighters. It eased his mind some to know at least several of his men had been soldiers during the Great War between the States.

Sam had sent four men and his foreman out to follow tracks. He was beginning to question the wisdom of that decision. Was it really necessary for him to know where the shooter had come onto his land and where he left it?

Sam was not sure how to answer that question and even began to wonder what it would prove. Sam turned and looked out the window as he mulled it over. He could see the old cottonwood tree up on the hill.

His thoughts turned to Johnny and how he had been bushwhacked at the watering hole. The small wage the average ranch hand was paid hardly seemed enough now. Sam paid a little better than most ranchers in the area and a lot better than some. Even that was not enough for a man to risk his life.

He also knew there wasn't a ranch hand in the country that didn't know what the risks of the job were from the very first day. When they took the job, they were expected to ride for the brand and do what was necessary to protect the brand's property from any and all threats. That's just the way it was, and the way it had always been.

Sam thought of Johnny and the sacrifice that he had made for the brand, his brand. He had a month's wages due him and it would now be paid to Helen. Somehow it seemed like too little for what Johnny had given to the Willard Ranch.

At that moment his thoughts were disturbed by the sound of horses coming toward the house. Sam stood up and walked to the door. He saw Casey and the four riders he had taken with him riding across the yard toward the barn. Only Casey veered off and turned toward the house.

As Sam stepped out on the porch to greet him, he glanced at his watch. It was already late afternoon. Time had gone by quickly. It wouldn't be long before Margaret would ring the dinner bell.

"How'd it go?" Sam asked as he looked up at Casey.

"Okay, boss. We split up at the place where we was shot at. I sent two of the hands to back-track the tracks that led up to that spot, and I took two of the hands and followed the tracks away from there.

"The shooter's tracks led south from where we was shot at to our property line, right to Frank Gregory's ranch. He had cut a openin' in the fence so's he could get onto the Gregory ranch. We fixed it before we come back."

"What about the one's that led up to where we were shot at? Where did the shooter come from?"

"Jack and Bill followed them. They said they come from up north. They lost the tracks about half way between the trees and our north property line. The ground was too hard and they lost them in the dried grass, but they got quite a ways 'for turnin' back to where we started."

"Interesting," Sam commented as he waited for Sam to finish.

"Yeah. It looked like the shooter had come in from the north and left out the south, kind a like someone that was crossin' the ranch and stopped to take a couple of shots at us as he was passin' through," Casey said.

"What are you saying, Casey?"

"I'm sayin' we have no better an idea of who we're lookin' for now then we did 'fore we left," Casey said, the disappointment showing in his voice and on his face.

"You might be right. Has Bill been able to remember who was riding that horse yet?"

"Not so far, but he has come up with where he'd seen it," Casey said with a more positive tone in his voice.

"And where was that?" Sam asked with interest.

"He saw it at the barn raisin' over at Will Carter's place this past spring."

"At Carter's ranch?" Sam asked, a little surprised at the information.

"That's what he said, boss."

"That's north of us," Sam said thinking out loud.

"Sure is," Casey replied, wondering what was going on in Sam's head.

"Did he say who was riding it?"

"Nope. He hasn't remembered that yet."

"Tell him to keep trying to remember."

"Will do."

"Casey, after you put your horse up, I would like you to get all of Johnny's things together and bring them up to the house. I'm sure Miss Westerman would like to see them. There may be some things in his belonging that she might like to keep."

"Sure thing," Casey replied, then reined his horse around and trotted off toward the barn.

Sam stood on the porch and watched as Casey rode off. He wondered what was going on. Unless Bill could remember who was riding the horse, there was no telling who it belonged to. Most of the ranchers in the valley had been over at the barn raising.

The one thing Sam was sure of was there had been no strangers at the barn raising. That left two very distinct possibilities. Either the horse belonged to someone who lived in the valley, or whoever owned the horse stayed in hiding while the barn raising was going on.

Sam had not missed the fact the shooter had crossed from Carter's ranch to Gregory's ranch, but that fact alone really meant nothing. However, it did hint at the possibility the shooter knew both Carter and Gregory.

Although the most likely answer was that the horse belonged to someone who lived in the valley, Sam began to wonder if Will Carter might have had someone hiding on his property. It would not have been hard to do. He also wondered if the shooter had been hired by Carter and had been hiding out at Carter's ranch all the time. He knew Carter had some ranch hands with questionable backgrounds, but nothing anyone could prove.

Sam sort of shoved that idea to the back of his mind for a while, as he had nothing solid to go on. He would have to think on it some more later.

He took one quick look around his ranch before he went back inside. The men were keeping good watch over the place. It would not be long before it would be time for dinner, but there were a couple of things Sam needed to do before dinner.

Sam turned and went into the house. Returning to his desk, he sat down to finish his paperwork. When he was finished, he wrote a letter to the Territorial Marshal in the hope of getting him to come here. It was his hope the Marshal's presence would help keep a lid on things until it all blew over, or things settled down again. Sam knew he couldn't count on the local sheriff to do anything. Under the circumstances, outside help was needed.

Just as Sam was finishing his letter to Marshal Franklin, he heard Helen come into the room. He looked up and smiled at her. She looked as if her afternoon nap might have picked up her spirits a little.

Helen had changed her clothes. She was now wearing a nice pair of tailored riding slacks like those worn by some of the more fashion conscious women back east. They accented the shapely curves of her hips. Her blouse looked very nice and very feminine, and was far more flattering to her figure than the shirt she had worn earlier.

"Hi. Did you get some rest?" Sam asked.

"Yes, I did. Thank you."

"Dinner will be ready in a little while."

"I really think I should be going. I've imposed on you enough. I do want to thank you for your time and your hospitality," she replied.

"Going? Going where?" Sam asked, somewhat surprised that she was planning on leaving so soon.

"Back to Ohio. I found what I came for," she replied, hoping he would ask her to stay.

"We can't let you leave on an empty stomach. It wouldn't be polite. Won't you reconsider staying and having a meal with us? Besides, I have Casey gathering up your brother's things."

"Oh, I hadn't thought about that," she said, her expression suddenly turning sad at the mention of her brother.

Just then Casey came up to the door. He was carrying two saddlebags and a carpetbag. Casey had a gun belt over his shoulder and a rifle tucked in the crook of his arm. He knocked on the door with his foot.

"Come in, Casey," Sam said as he went to the door and opened it for him.

"Where would yah like these thin's, Ma'am?" Casey asked.

"Put them in the guest room for now, Casey," Sam said before Helen had a chance to say anything. "Miss Westerman might like a little privacy while she sorts through Johnny's things."

Casey simply nodded his head and carried the things down the hall to the guest room.

"Thank you for your consideration of my feelings, Mr. Willard."

"Your welcome, but won't you please call me, Sam?" he asked again.

"Of course," she replied with a smile. "If you will call me, Helen."

Sam was looking at Helen when Margaret came into the living room. "Dinner is ready in the dining room. Is Casey eating with you?"

"Yes, he is, and so are you," Sam said as Casey returned to the living room. "Come on, Casey, you're eating here with us."

Casey nodded and stepped back making room for Sam and Helen. Sam took Helen by the arm and guided her into the dining room with Casey following along behind.

Once they had all sat down at the table, Margaret began passing the food around. When everyone had filled their plates, they began to eat. No one said anything for some time.

Sam liked having Helen sitting across the table from him. There was something about her that made him want to see her stay. He was hoping she might consider staying a little longer so he might get to know her.

"Excuse me, Miss Westerman, but."

"Please, call me, Helen," she interrupted with a smile.

"Okay, Helen," he said returning her smile. "I don't mean to be prying into your business, but have you made plans as to where you will stay the night tonight?" Sam said.

"Not really, but I'm sure there is some place in town where I could stay."

"Mrs. Barker has a boardin' house in town," Casey volunteered.

"Yes. Yes she does, but I don't think it's a good idea for you to return to town this late in the day," Sam said.

"I'm sure I will be all right. I doubt anyone is going to cause me any trouble."

"Under normal circumstances I would probably agree with you, but things are not normal around here right now. Besides it will be pretty close to dark by the time you get back to town," Sam pointed out.

Helen had not thought of that. It was clear what Sam had to say was quickly becoming a concern to her.

"Might I suggest you stay here?" Sam said not knowing how she would take such an invitation.

"I don't want to be any trouble," Helen replied as she looked across the table at Sam.

Helen wanted to stay and hoped Sam would find it no trouble to have her around. She wanted to get to know him better, but she didn't want to be hanging around not doing her share.

"It will be no trouble at all. You can use the same room you've been using."

Helen looked first at Casey and then at Margaret. Sam had given her the opportunity to stay, but she was not sure what the others might think if she stayed under the same roof as Sam.

"It's no trouble at all," Margaret agreed. "It would be nice to have another woman around for a little while."

"There, it's settled. You can stay as long as you want," Sam said with a smile.

"Okay," Helen conceded with a smile. "I'll stay under one condition."

"What's that?" Sam asked, curious as to what kind of a condition she could put on his invitation.

"That I can be of some help around here."

Sam looked at Casey, then at Margaret. They looked as if they might not mind having Helen stay.

"Okay, you've got a deal. How would it be if you help Margaret feed the ranch hands? She has a whole crew to feed everyday in the dining hall off the kitchen."

"That would be fine," Helen said with a smile as she looked at Sam.

Everyone seemed satisfied with the arrangement, especially Sam. As he continued to eat his meal, he found himself glancing at Helen from time to time. He even caught her glancing at him occasionally. Sam tried not to embarrass himself by making a strong effort to avoid staring at her. Nothing much else was said except for small talk during the remainder of dinner.

Helen had golden hair that hung down her back. Her blue eyes sparkled in the light, and her skin looked smooth and flawless. She had a very nice figure that Sam had not missed when she first arrived wearing jeans and a flannel shirt. He could not remember when there had been a prettier woman on the ranch, or a woman he found so interesting.

Helen was obviously a woman of courage and determination. She had proven that by traveling all the way from Ohio to find her brother.

When everyone was finished eating, Sam and Casey excused themselves while Helen helped

Margaret clear the table. Helen also helped Margaret clean up and put things away in the kitchen.

CHAPTER THIRTEEN

After dinner, Sam and Casey went out on the front porch of the ranch house while Margaret and Helen cleared the table and cleaned up the kitchen. Casey leaned against one of the porch pillars and began rolling himself a cigarette.

Sam leaned back against one of the other pillars and just looked out over the ranch yard. Sam was busy thinking about Helen and how good it made him feel when she had agreed to stay a little while longer. Neither of them spoke for several minutes. Finally, Sam broke the silence.

"What do you think of her?"

"What, boss?" Casey asked as he had not been paying attention.

Sam turned and looked at Casey. Casey was lighting his freshly rolled cigarette. Sam waited until he had it lit, then asked him again.

"What do you think of Miss Westerman?"

"Oh, she seems nice enough," Casey said, and then stopped to take a draw on his cigarette.

"I'll say this, she's a mighty fine lookin' woman," Casey added with a grin.

"Yeah, I noticed," Sam agreed with a grin. "She is that."

"She is what?"

Sam and Casey quickly straightened up and turned around. They discovered Helen was standing behind them at the door. They looked at each other and wondered how much of their conversation she had overheard. Needless to say, Sam was feeling a little uncomfortable and looked it.

Knowing they had been caught, Casey saw no reason to try to lie their way out of it. On the other hand, there was no reason to make himself look bad, either.

"Sam was just sayin' you're a mighty pretty woman," Casey said with a grin. "And I have to agree."

Sam looked over at Casey. He was rather surprised and embarrassed that Casey, his long time friend, would say that to her. After all, it had been Casey who had said she was a mighty fine looking women. He had simply agreed.

"Well, thank you," Helen said as she looked at Sam and smiled politely. "A woman always likes to know she is thought of as pretty, especially when those talking about her don't know she can hear them."

Helen could see Sam's face was a little red. He looked like he might be wishing there was a place close by where he could go and hide.

"Well, I best make my rounds and make sure all is secure," Casey said as he touched the brim of his hat, nodded slightly toward Helen, then turned and stepped off the porch.

Sam watched as Casey walked off toward the barn. He was wishing he was going with him. Now that Sam had been left alone with Helen, he wasn't sure what he should say to her. He already felt as if he had put his boot in his mouth.

Helen walked up next to Sam and leaned against the porch railing. She stood only a few inches away from him and looked out over the ranch yard. She didn't say anything for a moment or two. The silence was almost deafening to Sam.

"I'm sorry if I embarrassed you," Helen said smiling, but she didn't turn to look at him.

"That's okay. I'm sure I'll survive," Sam said still looking out over the ranch yard.

"This is a very nice ranch. I can see why Johnny wanted to work here," she said, hoping by changing the subject Sam might feel a little more comfortable. It seemed to work.

"Yes, it is nice here," Sam replied, a bit of pride in his voice.

Slowly, Sam turned and looked at Helen. The setting sun sparkled in her golden hair and glowed off her smooth tanned cheeks. Sam had an urge to reach out, take her in his arms and kiss her. No matter how much he wanted to, he didn't think it was a very good idea. After all, he hardly knew her, and had no idea what her reaction might be. He quickly decided it would be better if he took a little time to get to know her first.

"Would you like to see more of the ranch?" he asked hoping her answer would be yes.

"I'd love to," Helen replied as she turned and looked at him.

"It's not as nice around here this time of year as it is in the spring when all the prairie flowers are in bloom, but it still looks pretty nice."

"Yes, it does. I hear you have a new colt?"

"A filly, actually. But, yes, we do. If you like, we can go see her."

"I'd like that," she replied with a smile as she looked up at Sam's face.

Sam pushed himself away from the railing and reached out a hand to her. She looked down at his hand briefly, then looked up at him again. Helen smiled as she reached out and took hold of his hand. She let him lead her off the porch.

Hand in hand, they walked across the yard toward the barn. Neither of them said anything, they simply enjoyed being close to each other. The fact she had taken his hand and didn't let go of it made Sam think she might like him.

Helen didn't know what to think about Sam. She watched him out of the corner of her eye. There was no question in her mind he was handsome. His dark hair was wavy and his dark eyes sparkled whenever he talked about things he liked, such as the ranch. She had noticed his eyes sparkled when he talked to her. That thought pleased her, as she liked him, too.

He was tall and his long legs could make for long strides. She had seen him walk across the ranch yard before. He could cover the distance very quickly, but he seemed to take a slower pace when he was walking with her. That also pleased her. It told her that he could be patient and it showed his concern for her.

Sam couldn't help but notice Helen's hand was soft and small, yet it had a certain strength to it. He quickly found he liked holding her hand and being beside her.

As they walked into the barn, they passed the stall where Helen's horse had been put up for the night. She stopped briefly in front of the stall and reached out with her free hand to touch the horse on the nose. Sam continued to hold her other hand as he waited for her to gently rub the horse's nose.

"By the way, I meant to thank you for having your men take care of my horse."

"No problem. She's a good horse and seems to be comfortable here," Sam said.

"Yes, she does. She seems to be getting along with your black stallion very well."

"Midnight does seem to like her," Sam agreed with a grin.

Helen quickly realized they were talking about their horses, but could have just as easily been talking about themselves. In a way, she hoped they were.

When they got to the last stall in the barn, Sam let go of Helen's hand and slipped his hand around to the small of her back. He then guided her up to the gate of the stall.

Helen stepped up on the bottom rail of the gate so she could lean over the top and see the filly. Sam leaned against the gate as she looked over the boards of the stall. The new filly was standing on long spindly legs next to her mother. She was enjoying a good warm meal.

The filly's mother casually turned her head and looked toward Helen. Realizing there was no danger to her young one, she returned to eating her own dinner.

"Isn't she cute," Helen said as she watched the filly eat.

"She will be a good looking horse. She's got a good blood line," Sam said as he rested his arms on the top of the gate and looked into the stall to admire the filly.

"I can see that," Helen said as she turned and looked into Sam's eyes.

Sam was looking at her. She became so self-conscious about the way he was looking at her that she felt as if he was looking into her soul. It made her feel very uncomfortable as well as a bit nervous.

As Helen began to step down off the gate, her foot slipped causing her to fall off the stall gate toward Sam. She threw her arms around Sam's neck in an effort to break her fall and suddenly found herself wrapped in Sam's arms.

Her body was pressed tightly against him. She could almost hear her own heart beating. It had never happened to her before. There was something about being so close to Sam that disturbed every nerve in her body. The feel of her breasts pressed against his muscular chest sent a rush of desire through her that she was having difficulty controlling.

Sam held her close, his arms holding her tightly against him. He could feel the firmness of her breasts against his chest. He looked into her blue eyes as she looked up at him. Their lips were only inches away from each other.

The desire to kiss her while he held her tightly was almost more than Sam could stand. He looked into her eyes as he started to slowly move closer to her, but stopped when he heard a noise behind them.

Helen was staring into his eyes, patiently waiting and even hoping Sam would kiss her when her senses were disturbed by the same noise he had heard. She swallowed hard and let out a sigh of disappointment. She reluctantly slid her hands from around his neck and down onto his chest. She hesitated to push herself away from him, but straightened up.

Sam stood in front of her as she took a couple of deep breaths in an effort to regain control of her emotions. She was a little flushed.

Since her blouse had come loose at her waist, Sam gave her a few seconds to straighten out her clothes. He remained standing in front of her so whoever had come into barn might not be able to see her adjust her clothes. When she was ready, she looked up at him.

"Thank you," she whispered.

"You're welcome," he whispered, then turned around to see who had come into the barn.

"Margaret, what are you doing out here?" Sam asked, surprised to see her.

"Casey told me to find you. He and a couple of the hands are going up on the hill where they laid Johnny to rest. It seems Bill saw something move up there in the moonlight."

"Thank you, Margaret. Would you please escort Helen back to the house?"

"Yes, sir."

Without any delay, Sam left the barn and walked around to the corral where Bill had been standing guard. He glanced back over his shoulder to make sure Margaret and Helen were on their way to the house where they would be safe. As soon as he saw them enter the house, he turned his attention to finding Bill.

When Sam came around the back corner of the barn, he could see Bill over next to the board fence that formed one of the corrals behind the barn. He had his rifle resting on the top of a fence post. It was pointed toward the old cottonwood near the top of the hill.

"What's going on, Bill?"

"I thought I saw someone moving around up there by the cottonwood on the ridge. Casey and a couple of the guys are working their way up there to check it out," Bill said as he continued to look up toward the ridge.

"Where are the guys now?"

"They're moving up to the ridge from the northeast side of the hill. Casey told me to keep my eyes open, but don't shoot."

"Are you sure you saw something?"

"Yes, sir, but I can't be sure what. It could have been a man, I'm just not sure. I figured it was better to be safe than sorry, sir," Bill said without turning to look at Sam.

"Yeah, you're right. Keep an eye out," Sam said as he continued to watch for any sign of movement up on the hill.

As Sam leaned against the corral, he began to wonder what anyone would be doing up on the ridge at this late hour. It was certainly too far away for

164

anyone to be able to see anything around the ranch yard with it as dark as it was. At that distance, they wouldn't even be able to see where the guards were posted.

It was quiet and dark. There was only a little moonlight filtering out onto the open land. Sam was beginning to wonder how Bill could have seen anything that far away.

"Are you sure you saw something?" Sam asked.

"Yes, sir. It was a shadow or movement out there, but I saw it," Bill replied, confident that he had seen something.

Just then they could hear the sound of a horse running across the dry hard ground. It took only a moment or two before the sound faded away. On a clear night like this, sounds tended to carry for a long ways.

Although Sam had heard the sound of a horse, he could not see one. He stood at the corral and kept a watch up toward the cottonwood tree. It wasn't long before he heard the sounds of several men walking toward the barn. When they got close, he could make out Casey and a couple of the ranch hands.

"You see anything?" Sam asked.

"No, sir, but there was someone up there all right. Good eye." Casey said as he reached out and patted Bill on the shoulder as he passed him.

"Good job, Bill," Sam said as he turned and started off across the yard with Casey.

"Someone was up there, all right, but I don't know who or why."

"Did you see anything at all?"

"Just a shadow of someone ridin' off. He was headed south toward the Gregory place. Too darn dark tonight to see who it was," Casey said with a hint of disgust and disappointment in his voice.

"Well, at least whoever it was will know we are not sleeping. They will know we have guards out and about," Sam said as a way of giving something positive for Casey to think about.

"Yeah, they know that all right."

"I think you best get some rest. I'll see you in the morning."

"Okay, boss," Casey said, then turned and headed toward the bunkhouse.

Sam stopped in his tracks and watched Casey as he walked away. He stood there for a few minutes to think. Maybe in the morning he would ride up on the ridge and see if he could pick up any tracks. If they were lucky, they might be able to tell if it was the same rider that had taken a shot at them earlier in the day.

With the current crisis over, Sam found his thoughts returning to Helen. He had sent her to the house with Margaret. He was sure she would be worried not knowing what was going on.

He started toward the house again. As he approached the porch, he could see Helen and Margaret at the window. He waved casually at them as he stepped up on the porch.

"All's quiet," he said as he entered the house. "I think it would be a good idea if we all got some rest. Morning comes early around here."

"That's probably a good idea," Helen agreed with a smile.

"I'll see you in the morning," Sam said to Helen.

Helen nodded slightly, then turned and started down the hall to her room. Sam watched her for a moment as she walked away before he went over to his desk.

He folded the letter he had written earlier and put it in an envelope. Sam decided he would take it into town in the morning for posting. With that done, he walked down the hall to his room and turned in for the night.

CHAPTER FOURTEEN

It was still dark outside when Sam went into the kitchen to get his breakfast. He caught a glimpse of Helen as she left the kitchen carrying a large plate of bacon and a large bowl of scrambled eggs out to the dining hall where the ranch hands ate their meals.

Margaret was standing at the wood burning stove flipping flapjacks on the griddle and stacking those that were ready on a serving plate. Sam watched Margaret while he waited for Helen to return to the kitchen. For the first time he found it interesting to watch her prepare breakfast for the men. He had not realized how difficult a job it was for one person. Having Helen to help carry the food into the dining room saved Margaret a lot of walking, to say nothing of the other things Helen did to help.

"Good morning," he said as Helen came back into the kitchen.

"Good morning, Sam," she replied with a smile as she wiped her hands on the apron Margaret had loaned her.

"I see Margaret found you something to do."

"Yes, she has. You have a hungry crew here."

"Yes, we do, and if you don't get them fed, we will all be in big trouble," Margaret said with a grin.

"I guess I had better get back to work before the boss fires me," Helen said with a smile, then turned and picked up the plate of flapjacks.

Sam didn't say anything. He simply smiled and watched as Helen returned to the duties of feeding the men. Helen was not only a good-looking woman, she was a willing worker. Sam knew that was important on a ranch.

Sam went over to a table and picked up a plate for himself. He put some bacon and eggs, and a couple of flapjacks on it for his breakfast. With the full plate in one hand and a hot cup of coffee in the other, he went back into the ranch house dining room to eat alone. Sam had a lot on his mind. Casey would let the men know what was on tap for the day. He felt if he ate alone, he would have time to think a few things out.

Before he started eating, he spread out his map on the dining room table. While he ate, he looked over the map of the ranch and the rest of the valley. He thought about what had happened over the past few days. He took a pencil and drew circles on the map where each incident had taken place. He marked where his men were and where the shooter had been. Once he had them all marked out, he sat and stared at the map as if looking for some sort of pattern.

There had been five attacks directed at Sam or his men. Of the five attacks, one had taken place in town and had turned into a shootout in the back alley. Of the remaining four, only twice had shots been fired at a distance considered far greater than one could expect the average saddle rifle to reach with any degree of accuracy. Only once had a 40-60 Caliber rifle been used at a range when almost any gun would have done the job. At each of those three locations, they had found the brass casings from a 40-60 caliber rifle. In only one of the five incidents was a Winchester 30-30 used. The Winchester 30-30 was the most common saddle rifle in the area. Almost everyone in the valley had one.

Since most men prefer to use one gun over another and usually stuck with the one they felt the most comfortable using, Sam was convinced there were at least two people taking shots at him and his men. At the moment, Sam had no idea what that piece of information meant, but he was sure it had some meaning for him. He was determined to find out who was shooting at him and his men no matter how many shooters were involved.

Sam's thoughts were suddenly interrupted when Casey came into the dining room. Sam stopped and looked up at him.

"Morning, Casey."

"Mornin', boss. I got a report there are some of Will Carter's cattle on our range and drinkin' our water. What do you want me to do about it?"

"How'd they get on our range?"

"Someone cut the fence, I would guess. One of the hands discovered the cattle while checkin' waterin' holes."

"I want you to take a few men and round up Carter's cattle. Run them back across to his property and fix the fence."

"Yes sir."

"Casey, you be careful out there. Avoid getting into a fight with anyone if you can, you understand?"

"Yeah," Casey replied.

"Defend yourself, but don't start anything. And keep a sharp lookout. Whoever is doing the shooting is getting more and more determined, and more willing to shoot at us."

"Got it, boss."

"We'll probably have to start riding fence. Work out a schedule for the men. Have them ride in groups of at least four when riding fence."

"Okay. I'll take three with me and take care of that problem. We'll check the fence along the north today."

"Okay, but keep your eyes open. We don't need to bury any more of the hands."

"Right."

Sam watched as Casey turned and left the dining room. Sam knew Casey was as good a ranch hand as they came. He was also a good foreman. He would do whatever it took to get the job done.

With that taken care of, Sam returned to his map. As his eyes passed over the map and fell on the Gregory ranch, he remembered what it was he was supposed to have done last night. He remembered he was supposed have met Marie at the old oak tree on their property line last night at nine, but he forgot all about it.

He didn't like the fact he had forgotten. It made him feel as if he was breaking his word. It didn't matter that it was her idea. He never liked breaking a promise, but in this case he was not sorry he didn't go.

The more he thought about Marie, the more he felt there was really nothing between them. He was beginning to think there probably never had been. At least there was nothing two people could build a lasting and loving relationship on.

Sam began to wonder if he felt that way because Helen had come into his life. He liked Helen, and he was sure she liked him. Sam knew Helen had nothing to do with him forgetting to meet Marie. He had told himself the other day, even before he met Helen, Marie was not right for him.

As Sam sipped his coffee, he understood that if he really cared for Marie he would not have forgotten she wanted him to meet her. With that firmly settled in his mind, he turned his thoughts to other things, such as his ride into town.

He had told his men they were not to ride anywhere alone. It was necessary for him to do the same if he expected his men to do it. Besides, he didn't want another incident like the one on his last trip into town. He would get a couple of men together and go into town to report another shooting to Sheriff Becker. He would also report the cut fence and post his letter.

He knew it wouldn't do any good to talk to the sheriff about what was happening at his ranch, but he did want to know what Jake or Doc Miller had found out about the two men who tried to kill him. He also wanted to mail his letter off to the Territorial Marshal.

Helen interrupted his thoughts as she came into the dining room. She was holding a pot of coffee.

"I thought I would check and see if you needed more coffee."

"Oh, yes. Thank you."

Sam leaned back in his chair and watched her as she stepped up close to him and leaned over to pour some hot coffee in his cup. He found it hard not to watch her every move. She seemed to move with grace, like a woman with confidence in herself.

"I have to go into Shallow Creek today. Would you like to come along?"

She straightened up and looked down at him. Helen was surprised he would ask her, but glad he did.

"I thought you might like to pick up a few things while we're in town," Sam added, hoping she could see the logic in her going with him.

"Well, I did leave a few things with Mr. Potter at the general store. It would be nice to have a few more clothes to wear since I'm staying here. I do need to get some material to make a couple of aprons, too. I can't keep borrowing Margaret's," she replied.

"Good. We can take the buckboard and pick them up."

"I only brought a couple of carpet bags with me. Most of my things are in storage back in Ohio. It really won't be necessary to take a buckboard. When are we going?"

"It will be light before long. We'll go then. I have a few things to take care of first."

"I'll be ready," she replied, and then returned to the kitchen.

Sam was pleased she wanted to go into town with him. It didn't make any difference to him that she wanted to pick up her luggage, or that she wanted to purchase some material for aprons. He wanted to spend time with her. The fact there would be other riders with them didn't dampen his prospects of going riding with her, either.

Helen went out to the kitchen with a little bit of a bounce to her step. She was delighted she would be able to spend a good part of the day with Sam. She

174

liked him and liked being around him. The fact they
would be escorted into town by several of the ranch
hands as guards didn't discourage her or her desire
to spend what time she could with Sam, either.

As soon as Helen was finished in the kitchen, she
went out to the barn and walked up to her horse.
After rubbing her hand over the horse's nose, she
reached for the bridle on the peg next to the stall.
She opened the stall and stepped up in front of her
horse. As she slipped the bridle over the horse's
head, she whispered to it.

"We're going for a ride this morning. Would
you like to go to town with Midnight?"

The Palomino bobbed its head up and down.
Helen could not help but smile. Her horse seemed
as excited as she was, and was ready to go, too.

As she was leading her horse out of the stall,
Sam came into the barn. He smiled when he saw
the two of them. He took a moment to admire them.
They both had beautiful long blond manes, he
thought as he moved closer. They were both trim
and nicely built and seemed to be right for each
other. He found it hard to take his eyes off Helen,
but since he didn't want to startle her, he thought it
would be best if he said something.

"Would you like me to help you saddle your
horse," he asked as he moved closer.

"No, that won't be necessary," she replied as she glanced over her shoulder at Sam. "I can do it, but thanks for offering."

"Your horse seems ready to go," Sam said with a smile as he walked toward the stall where Midnight was standing.

"Yes. She's always ready to go for a ride. She seems to like to go in the morning when it's cool."

"Midnight's the same way. He likes an early morning run," Sam said as he took Midnight's bridle off the peg and opened the gate to the stall.

"Does your horse have a name," Sam asked from inside the stall as he slipped the bridle over Midnight's head.

"Yes. Her name is Sunshine because of her golden color," Helen said as she continued to saddle her horse.

"Nice name. Fits her," Sam said, as he led the big stallion out of the stall.

"Midnight is a good name for your horse, too."

Sam tied Midnight to a post, and then finished saddling him. It wasn't long before he was ready. When he was finished, he led his horse out of the barn. Helen walked along side him leading her horse. They didn't say anything as they walked up to the house and tied their horses out in front.

"Are we ready to go?" Helen asked.

"Not just yet. There will be a couple of hands riding with us this morning. They'll be along in a minute."

"I wasn't being nosey, but I couldn't help but notice the map you had laid out on the dining room table this morning. I was wondering what the map was?"

"That's a map of the valley. I drew it up a few years back. It shows where all the ranches are and where the rivers and creeks run. It also shows where all the watering holes are located, at least the ones on this ranch. It helps when we want to move cattle from one place to another. We can figure out where to move them."

"I noticed you had made some marks on it, what are those for?"

"They're the places where we have had attacks made on us in the last few days," he said as he looked at her, not knowing how she would react.

"How many have there been?"

"Five, so far."

"You sound like you might be expecting more?"

"Yes. I'm afraid I am. If we don't get a good amount of rain soon, I believe things will get a lot worse around here before they get any better."

Helen looked at him. She didn't say anything more. It was clear from the look in Sam's eyes that he expected more trouble. She wished it would not be so, but she was smart enough to know there was little chance of improvement in the current situation without a big change in the weather.

Sam was deep in thought when he heard several horses plodding across the dry hard ground of the yard. He looked up to see four of his men, all of them well armed with pistols and rifles, coming toward the house. He straightened up and turned toward Helen.

"Our escort is here," he said.

Helen was watching the four men as they came across the yard from the corral. Seeing them with rifles held in their hands as they sat on their horses reminded her of how things were. It even frightened her a little. It made it very clear that this was not just a pleasant ride into town they were taking.

"You ready?" Sam asked as he looked at her.

Sam could see the worried look in her eyes. He was wondering if it was a good idea to take her with him to town. He had asked her to go with him, but he was having second thoughts about it now.

"You don't have to go if you don't want to," Sam said softly. "We can pick up your things at the general store for you."

Helen turned and looked at him. She could see the worried look on Sam's face. It was at that moment she realized he was beginning to understand a little of how she must feel.

"No, I want to go," she said, determined not to let him know she was worried, too.

"Okay," he said as he stepped off the porch and untied his horse from the hitching rail.

He waited for Helen to get mounted before he put his foot in the stirrup and swung himself into the saddle. He then reined his horse around and started down the lane.

Helen rode up along side Sam while the four ranch hands fell in behind them. When they reached the end of the lane, Sam kicked his horse into a steady but easy gait that was also easy for Helen's smaller horse and for the other riders.

There was little said on the way into town. Everyone was watching for anything that might cause them harm. The ride to Shallow Creek turned out to be peaceful and quiet.

CHAPTER FIFTEEN

Sam and Helen rode side by side into the quiet little town of Shallow Creek with their escort of four of Sam's ranch hands close behind them. The sun-baked street was empty except for the buggy in front of Potter's General Store and a couple of horses in front of the Red Garter Saloon.

As the riders slowly moved down the street, Sam stared at the buggy. He was sure it was the one he had seen Frank Gregory and his granddaughter use the other day. It crossed his mind they might be in town. He had hoped he would not run into Marie today, but it was becoming apparent that was not going to be the case.

Sam turned and reined up in front of the Sheriff's Office. Helen turned and moved up along side him. As Sam sat in the saddle, his ranch hands spread out on either side of them forming a line of well armed men in front of the Sheriff's Office.

Sam looked around and found the street was empty, but it was the middle of the week and it was already getting hot. It was especially hot for so early in the day. He turned in his saddle and looked at his ranch hands while they waited for instructions.

"Jack, you and Bill take Miss Westerman to the general store and help her get her things. Don't start anything and keep your eyes open. I don't want any trouble, but protect yourself and Miss Westerman."

"Yes, sir," Jack replied.

"Helen, I'll meet you in the general store in a little while. I have to talk to the sheriff."

Helen replied with a slight nod.

"The rest of you wait here with me," Sam added.

Helen looked a little worried. The seriousness showing on Sam's face and the way he gave his instructions reminded her of her father who had been an officer in the Union Army. She had seen him give orders to his troops in much the same way. Although this was not a war between two countries, she understood it was fast becoming a war of survival. Things were very unstable here in the valley and there was little hope it would get any better very soon.

Helen wanted to wait for Sam, but she reined her horse around. She started toward the general store as Sam had instructed along with Jack and Bill, one on either side of her.

Sam watched as his ranch hands escorted Helen to Potter's General Store. Sam's attention was quickly drawn to the front of the Sheriff's Office by the sound of the door opening.

Sheriff Becker stepped out onto the boardwalk and looked at Sam and his men as they sat in their saddles. Becker didn't seem to be in any hurry to say anything. It was a moment or so before he spoke.

"Well, I see you brought a couple of your hired gunmen with you this time," Becker said as he casually leaned back against the door frame to his office, crossed his arms in front of him and looked up at Sam.

Sam wanted to step out of the saddle and wipe the smug look off his face, but he knew it would give Becker the excuse he needed to arrest him. He was not going to start a fight that would only end up in blood shed.

"They're not hired gunmen, but I'm sure they're quite capable of taking care of themselves should the need arise," Sam said, the sound of his voice showing he had confidence in his men's ability, as well as their loyalty.

"Who's the pretty little thing that came into town with you?" Becker asked as he glanced down the street.

"She is the sister of one of my ranch hands. Her brother was shot in the back by some coward while he was checking watering holes," Sam said as he watched Becker for some sort of reaction.

"I suppose you're comforting her," Becker said with a lewd grin.

"You would think that," Sam retorted sharply. "I'm only here to let you know there has been a killing on my place, but I don't know why I waste my time with you. Since you've been bought and paid for, I know you won't do anything about it."

"You saying that I'm owned?" Becker asked sharply as the expression on his face showed his growing anger.

Sam watched him as he straightened up and dropped his hands to his sides. It sort of surprised Sam that he had actually touched on a nerve, something he didn't think Becker had.

"You best take that back," Becker insisted.

Sam noticed Becker was moving his fingers as if he was thinking about drawing against him for his comment.

"I wouldn't do anything stupid if I were you," Sam said, the tone of his voice warning Becker to be very careful about what he decided to do. "It wouldn't take much for me to kill you right where you're standing."

Becker looked from Sam to the two ranch hands sitting on their horses, one on each side of Sam, and each one with a rifle pointed in his general direction. It suddenly became vividly clear to Becker that he was in a very dangerous position. All Sam had to do was to give the word and his men would fill him so full of lead it would take half the town to carry his body to the cemetery.

Sweat began to run down Becker's face as he began to realize he was pushing his luck. He had threatened Willard, which he quickly decided had been the wrong thing to do. If he didn't tread carefully, he might not live to see the end of the day.

Sam sat in his saddle and watched Becker, almost hoping he would draw his gun. He was ready in case Becker got a little brave and a lot stupid, and tried to draw against him. It was easy for him to see how nervous Becker had become. After a moment or two, he noticed Becker relax a little and that he had apparently decided not to press his luck any further. It was clear Sam had his undivided attention.

"As I was saying, since you don't have the backbone to do anything about the shootings and the killing on my place, I'm sending for the Territorial Marshal, Jeb Franklin. Once Franklin gets here and takes over, you won't have any authority to do anything."

"He can't come in here and take over," Becker said.

It was clear by the look on Becker's face he didn't like the idea he might be replaced.

"He can and you know it. And if I know him, he will take over. And when that happens, you will be just another citizen," Sam said as he glared down at Becker while he waited for a reaction.

Sam continued to watch Becker very close. When it was clear Becker had nothing more to say, Sam pulled back on the reins of his horse. Midnight slowly backed away from the hitching rail. Without taking his eyes off Becker, Sam turned his horse, nudged him in the side and rode on down the street to Potter's General Store with his two ranch hands at his side.

Sheriff Becker stood in the doorway of his office and watched as Sam and his men rode away. Although he was watching them, his mind had quickly turned to thoughts of Marshal Franklin. The way Sam had talked about him made it sound like they might be old friends. Becker also knew that if Marshal Franklin came and took over, he would not have any authority to do anything and his life would not be worth a wooden nickel.

Sam reined up in front of the general store just as Marie was coming out. She stopped and smiled up at him. Sam didn't say anything, nor did he smile back at her. He simply swung down from the saddle and tied his horse to the hitching rail. He then turned and looked at Marie.

"Hi, Marie," he said casually and politely, then waited for her to say something.

"I'm a little upset with you, Sam," Marie said with a little girl hurt look on her face that soon turned to a soft pleasant smile. "But I forgive you."

"Forgive me for what?" he asked, his voice showing no emotion.

"For not meeting me like you were supposed to," she reminded him.

"Oh. I got busy," he replied without any indication of regret, or that he intended to explain why he had been too busy to meet her.

"Is that all you have to say to me?" she asked, a little surprised he was showing no feelings toward her at all.

"Yes."

"Something has upset you. What is it?"

Sam looked at her for a minute and thought about what he should say. He had remembered hearing somewhere what her grandfather did during the Civil War. Sam could see no reason to keep what he was thinking from her.

"Do you know what your grandfather did during the Civil War?" he asked looking her right in the eyes.

"What?" she asked with surprise. "Ah, well, yes. I know what he did, but what does that have to do with us?"

"What did he do?" Sam asked, ignoring her question.

"He fought for the South, why?"

"I know he fought for the South. What I want to know is what did he do?"

"Well, he was too old for the infantry so I believe he was something called a sharpshooter," she said, still looking a little confused by his question.

"A sharpshooter?"

"Yes. Why do you want to know what he did? The war is over."

There was only a slight change of expression on Marie's face. Sam could not understand what it meant. However, something in the back of his mind told him she knew what he was getting at.

"Sharpshooter is another way of saying sniper."

"Okay, but what's that have to do with us?" she asked, trying very hard to retain her composure.

"There has been a sharpshooter on my property. This sniper has not only shot at my men and me, but he killed one of my ranch hands. This sharpshooter shot him in the back like a coward. The man he killed was a nice young man who never hurt anyone."

"Are you saying that my grandfather killed him?" she asked bluntly with a tone of anger and surprise in her voice.

"No, but the tracks led right to his ranch."

"You're saying my grandfather shot a man in the back like a common coward," she insisted, her voice showing that she was now angry.

"No, I'm not. I said a sharpshooter shot one of my men in the back and then fled to your grandfather's ranch. I don't know if it was your grandfather."

"It's the same thing," she fired back at him.

"Not quite. If I had any proof at all your grandfather shot my ranch hand down in cold blood,

I wouldn't be standing here in front of the general store talking to you about it. I would be hunting your grandfather down. Then I would take him to the territorial capitol so I could watch him hang," Sam said, his voice showing his anger.

Marie stood there looking at him. Her eyes were as big as saucers and her mouth standing open. She had never seen this side of Sam. It frightened her. She was not sure if it frightened her because he was talking about her grandfather, or if it was because there was so much anger in Sam's eyes that she was convinced he meant every word he said. Whatever he meant, she was sure he would do whatever it took to find the sharpshooter.

Just then, Helen came out of the general store. She was carrying a couple of carpetbags. Helen was surprised to see the strange look on Sam's face as she walked toward him.

"Sam, are you all right?" she asked, her concern showing on her face and in her voice.

Sam turned and looked at her. His expression of anger gradually turned to a more pleasant smile. The fire in his eyes softened as he looked at her.

"Yes, I'm fine. Did you get your things?" he asked calmly.

"Who is this?" Marie interrupted, wondering what Sam was doing talking to this woman.

"This is Miss Westerman. She is the sister of the young man who was shot in the back by the sharpshooter," Sam said as he looked right at Marie.

"Hello," Helen said with a friendly smile.

"Helen, this is Miss Marie Gregory. Her grandfather owns the ranch south of mine."

"Oh," Helen replied as the smile disappeared from her face.

Helen didn't know what to think. She looked up at Sam wondering why he had introduced her to Marie, and what he expected her to say. Helen knew Sam had not been getting along with the owner of the ranch south of him, yet here he was introducing her to the owner's granddaughter.

"I have all my things," Helen finally said as she looked up at Sam. "I'm ready to return to the ranch whenever you are."

The expression on Helen's face told Sam that she wanted to leave as soon as possible. Sam took her carpetbags and hung one on his saddle and the other on her saddle. He then reached out a hand to her.

Helen took his hand and stepped up next to her horse. After slipping her foot into the stirrup, she swung herself into the saddle and looked down at Sam.

"I'll be with you in a minute. I have a letter to post," Sam said, then turned to go into the general store.

Helen watched as Sam turned around and walked into Potter's General Store. As soon as he disappeared inside the store, she turned her attention toward Marie.

Marie was glaring up at Helen. To Marie's way of thinking, she could easily see why Sam would be attracted to Helen. Although she hated to admit it, Helen was very pretty. She was also convinced Sam was no different than most men and she was convinced all men liked blondes.

Helen didn't know what to think of Marie. She was a pretty young woman. At least, she could be if she would smile a little. Helen got the feeling Marie did not like her, but why? Was she jealous because she was riding with Sam? Or was Marie angry because she was staying at the ranch with Sam? Maybe a little of both.

Suddenly, Marie turned sharply and stormed into the general store. She found Sam talking to John Potter, the owner.

"I need this letter to go out as soon as possible," Sam told John.

"It'll go out on tomorrow's stage," John assured him.

"Thanks," Sam replied, then turned to leave.

Sam stopped in his tracks when he saw Marie coming toward him. He could tell by the look in her eyes she was mad as hell, but it didn't matter to him one way or the other.

"Who is that woman?" Marie demanded.

"I told you who she is," Sam replied quietly.

"Is she living on your ranch?"

"Yes. She works for me. She is Margaret's helper around the ranch house and in the kitchen."

"I don't like it. Is she living in your house?" Marie demanded to know, her temper showing.

"Yes, she is. What did you expect? Should I make her sleep in the barn with the horses? Or perhaps you would prefer she sleep in the bunkhouse with the men?"

"I don't like her there at all," Marie blurted out angrily.

"I don't think it is any of your business. And I don't care if you like her there or not. I like her there and she is welcome to stay as long as she wants. Do I make myself clear?"

Sam didn't wait for a reply from her. He simply stepped aside and walked past her. He went out the front door of the store without a backward glance.

Marie turned around and caught a glimpse of his back as he walked out. If looks could kill, Sam would have been dead several times over. All Marie could think of was this woman had ruined her plans. Her chances of becoming the wife of the richest man in the valley were looking pretty dim at the moment. In shear frustration, she stomped her foot.

Marie suddenly realized John Potter was watching her. Her face turned red as a beet. Marie turned around and stormed back out the door going right to her buggy. As she came out on the street, she saw that Sam, the woman and his men were headed down the street toward the edge of town. She didn't wait to see where they went. Instead, she got into her buggy, turned the horse toward the other end of town and whipped the poor animal. She raced out of town as fast as the horse could go.

CHAPTER SIXTEEN

Sam didn't say anything to Helen as he turned his horse around and started toward the edge of town. He was sure Helen was curious about what Marie might have meant to him, but he had doubts in his own mind as to whether this was a good time to talk to her about it. Sam wanted to tell Helen that Marie meant nothing to him, but didn't know what to say or how to approach the subject.

Helen quickly moved up beside Sam so she could be near him in case he decided to talk to her. She could sense the tension within him.

When they were about half way back to the ranch, Sam remembered he had wanted to talk to Doc Miller and Jake about the two men that had tried to bushwhack him. The encounter with Marie had distracted him causing him to forget about it. He even thought about taking a couple of the men and going back, but it was too far. Besides, it didn't seem important at the moment. He had more important things on his mind right now. He could talk to them later.

Helen rode along side Sam all the way back to the ranch. Her mind was full of thoughts, as well as questions about the woman that she had met in town. She wondered what Marie meant to Sam, and what Sam meant to her.

Helen was sort of hoping Sam would say something about her, maybe even make it clear Marie meant nothing to him, but he remained silent. She liked Sam and wanted him to like her, but she didn't want to get in the way if he loved someone else.

Helen wanted to talk to Sam about Marie once they got back to the ranch where they could have some privacy. Instead, she decided it might be best to remain silent until Sam was ready to talk to her. The last thing she wanted was for Sam to think she was prying into his business or that she was being pushy.

During the rest of the day Helen didn't really make a concerted effort to avoid Sam. She simply tried to keep herself busy. When she was not working, she spent time in her room.

It was getting late when Helen decided she should check on her horse. She knew one of the ranch hands had taken her horse to the corral and had taken care of it when they returned from town. However, she was not sure if any of the ranch hands had put her horse in the barn for the night. She felt the need to make sure her horse had been fed and bedded down for the night before she went to bed.

As she stepped off the porch of the ranch house and started across the yard toward the barn, she saw someone standing next to the corral leaning against the fence. In the late evening dusk, she wasn't sure who it might be. At first, she thought it was one of the ranch hands standing guard, but remembered the guards usually stood closer to the back of the barn where they could see out across the prairie.

As she walked across the yard and got closer, she realized it was not one of the ranch hands. It was Sam. He was looking out across the corral toward the cottonwood trees along the dried creek bed. She wondered what he was doing and what he might be thinking about.

There was little doubt that Sam had a lot on his mind. After all there was the likelihood of a range war looming on the horizon. There was also the damage the drought was doing to his ranch as well as to the other ranches in the valley. Then there was the safety of his men, and, of course, there was Marie. Any or all of these things would be enough to keep a man's mind occupied for some time.

Since Sam had not confided in her, she thought about going back inside so she would not disturb him. However, she did feel a strong need to check on her horse. Her need to check on her horse won out. She walked as quietly as she could toward the barn hoping not to disturb Sam.

"Helen," Sam called out to her.

Helen stopped in her tracks, then slowly turned to look at him. She watched him as he walked toward her.

"Hi. I didn't mean to bother you. You looked as if you had something on your mind," she said as a way of apologizing for disturbing him.

"You aren't bothering me. What are you doing out here so late?" he asked.

"I was just going to check on my horse," she replied as she looked up at him.

"The hands have already taken care of her. She's already been fed and bedded down for the night."

"Oh," she replied, then waited as she was hoping he had more to say to her.

"I'll just go back in and leave you with your thoughts," she added when he didn't say anything more.

"Wait. Could we talk for a minute?" he asked rather shyly, his voice soft and unsure.

"It's getting rather late. I have to get up early," she said.

All day she had wanted him to talk to her. Now that he seemed ready to talk, she was not sure she wanted to hear what he had to say, especially if it was about Marie.

"I know, but I would really like to have a talk with you. It won't take long," he assured her.

"All right," she said, then waited for him to say something.

"Let's walk," he said as he took her gently by the arm.

Helen was patient with him. Now that she had agreed to listen to him, she wanted him to talk to her. The problem was he wasn't saying anything as they walked toward the barn. Finally, Sam broke the silence.

"I don't know how to say this," Sam said, the tone of his voice showing just a hint of his frustration.

He then stopped and turned in front of her.

"Just say what's on your mind. I'm a big girl"

Helen looked up at him. She was wondering what it was he needed to say to her that seemed to be so difficult for him.

"I would like to have you stay here on the ranch, but - - I think it might get rather dangerous around here."

"Then you want me to leave?" Helen asked with surprise.

"No, well, in a way. Damn it, you're making this hard," he blurted out.

Helen didn't say anything. She was confused about what he really wanted. Helen decided it was best if she just gave him time to gather his thoughts. She was afraid what he wanted to say might have something to do with Marie. Time passed slowly without a word from Sam. She couldn't wait any longer to find out. She had to know now.

"Does this have anything do with Marie?" Helen finally asked.

"No. Why would you think that?" Sam asked, surprised that Helen would even mention her.

"I saw the way she looked at you."

"I have no feelings for her," Sam said without a second of hesitation.

Helen let out a sigh of relief. He was not in love with Marie. However, it had been easy for her to tell Marie had her sights set on him.

"Maybe not, but she has feelings for you."

"I think the only feelings she has for me is this ranch."

"I don't understand?" Helen said, her voice showing she was confused by his comment.

Sam thought for a moment before he spoke. "Mind you, I don't know this for a fact, but I think she would like to get her claws into me because I have the largest ranch in the valley. I believe she thinks if she could get her hooks in me it would make her something special."

"Do you really believe that?"

"Yes, I think I do," he said a little surprised and relieved that he was finally able to put into words what he had felt for some time.

Helen was glad Sam was not interested in Marie. She had been worried for nothing.

"Helen," Sam said as he reached out and took hold of her by her arms.

He suddenly found it hard to speak to her as he looked into her eyes. She was looking up at him as if she was waiting for him to say something, but he didn't know what to say. He found her eyes sparkled in the dim moonlight and her lips looked so inviting. He had a deep burning desire to kiss her, right here, right now.

Helen could see the puzzled look on his face. The feel of his strong hands on her arms and his silence was causing her whole body to want him to take her in his arms and kiss her. She couldn't understand why he didn't.

Slowly, Sam drew her closer. He let go of her arms and quickly moved his large hands to her narrow waist. She slid her hands up his chest to his shoulders as he pulled her closer to him.

Helen could feel the strength of his hands as he drew her tightly against him. As she leaned against him, she tipped her head back and slid her hands around behind his neck. Running her fingers through his dark wavy hair, she drew him even closer, closing her eyes in anticipation of his lips meeting hers.

Sam bent down until their lips met in a hard passionate kiss. As they kissed, he slid his hands around to the small of her back and pressed her tightly against him.

It was a long passionate kiss that left them both breathless. Helen's heart pounded in her chest. Her whole body tingled with a deep longing for him.

She had never been kissed with such a burning need before, and she liked it.

Sam could feel the warmth of her firm breasts as she pressed herself against him. Their kiss sent waves of desire through him. He could not seem to get enough of her.

When their kiss ended, Helen did not let go of him. She simply leaned back, opened her eyes and looked up at him. She could see his love for her in his eyes, and she could feel his desire for her in the way he held her.

Sam looked down into her sparkling blue eyes. He could see she had liked the kiss they had shared. There was no doubt in his mind he had liked it. He had never kissed or been kissed like that before. It was a deep excitable kiss that contained all the love two people could muster for each other. He wanted her more than he had ever wanted anything before.

"I want you to stay," Sam whispered, still looking into her eyes and trying to catch his breath.

Helen did not say anything. She simply smiled up at him then laid her head against his strong chest. She could hardly believe what was happening to her. The feel of being in his strong arms as she rested her head on his chest filled her heart with joy. The sound of his heartbeat told her how much he wanted her.

Sam wasn't sure if he should say something to her or not. Just holding her in his arms was enough for the moment. He stood there and ran his hands up and down the smooth curves of her back, from her shoulders to the small of her back. He didn't want this moment to end. He had forgotten, at least for the moment, what it was he had wanted to talk to her about.

After a few minutes with her head on his chest, listening to his strong steady heartbeat, Helen lifted her head and looked back up at him. She didn't want this time to end, nor did she want to end the feel of his large strong hands on her back. Yet, they could not stand out here in front of the barn forever.

Gently and carefully, she slid her hands from his shoulders down to his chest. She gently pushed herself away from him as she smiled up at him.

"What would your ranch hands think if they were to see us like this?" she asked, still a little breathless.

"My guess is they would think I am one very lucky guy."

"I'm sure," she said with a soft chuckle. "But I think we should go in."

"Don't you want to check on your horse?"

"I don't know. Is it safe to go into the barn with you? You might try to take advantage of me," she said jokingly, but wishing he would.

"I might, but that's the chance you have to take," he replied with a grin.

"Then I'll go in the barn with you."

Sam slid his hand around behind her as he walked with her to the barn. Once inside the barn, he pulled her around behind the door and took her in his arms again.

Helen did not resist. She simply melted against him. She put her hands behind his head and pulled his face down until their lips met again. It was another long passionate kiss she could feel run through her entire body, exciting every nerve and making her want more of him.

Sam liked the feel of her as she returned his kiss with as much passion as he had shown her. He did not want this moment to be interrupted, but it was not to be. The sound of a horse running at full clip into the ranch yard drifted into the barn and into their consciousness alerting them that something was wrong.

Sam jerked himself away from her and turned around. He gently, but firmly, pushed her around behind him to protect her from any harm that might come their way. He drew his gun and stepped up close to the barn door.

"Mr. Willard, Mr. Willard," the rider called out as he reined his horse to a stop in the ranch yard.

"What is it," Sam asked as he stepped out of the barn with Helen right behind him.

"Casey's been hurt. He's hurt real bad, Mr. Willard," the young ranch hand said, his voice showing how excited he was.

"Where is he?"

"He's out in the west pasture. Jacob and Joe are with him."

"How bad's he hurt?"

"Real bad, Mr. Willard. They hurt him bad. Jacob sent me to find you and to get a wagon."

Several of the men had come running when they heard the shouting and the news that Casey was hurt.

"Jack, hitch up the wagon. You, get a fresh horse," Sam said to the rider.

"Yes, sir," the rider said, then took his horse to the corral.

Sam picked out several men to ride with him and instructed them to get their guns. He instructed the others to arm themselves and to keep watch over the place in case it was a trick to get them away from the ranch house.

"I'll get some bandages and a blanket," Helen said as she started for the house.

Sam didn't say anything to her. He simply watched her as she ran toward the ranch house. By the time she returned from the ranch house, the wagon was ready. Margaret was with her carrying several blankets.

The women spread out the blankets in the bottom of the wagon to make a bed. Helen had pieces of cloth to make bandages and a jug of water to help clean any wounds Casey might have.

Sam helped load the blankets in the wagon. As he did, he noticed Helen had taken time to strap on the handgun that had belonged to her brother.

"I can't let you go. It's too dangerous," he said as he grabbed her by the arm.

"I'm going," she insisted while looking him in the eye. "I can help him."

Sam looked into her eyes. She was determined to go. He felt a twinge of pride in her for her courage, but he also knew it could be hazardous.

"All right, but you stay close to me," he insisted.

"Don't worry, I will," she said as he helped her into the wagon.

As soon as Sam was in the wagon, they all started out. It was dark and that meant it would be slow going. To rush on out across the prairie in the dark in a wagon would do no one any good, especially Casey. If they wrecked the wagon or crippled a horse, it would just take more time to get to Casey. It was a long way to the west pasture and with the wagon it would probably take most, if not all of the rest of the night.

The wagon bounced along the hard dry ground. There was no trail to follow, only wide-open prairie to cross. The fact that the moon was almost full and the sky was clear made it possible to travel. It was the first time in months Sam was glad there were no clouds in the sky.

Helen sat close to Sam. She rested one hand on his leg and held onto the wagon seat with the other. There was nothing she could do for now but wait until they got to Casey, and to pray.

"He'll be okay," she said, more to reassure herself than for Sam's benefit.

"I know. He's a tough old buzzard," Sam said as he glanced over at her, then turned back to watch where he was going."

Nothing else was said as they moved across the prairie as fast as they dared. It seemed to take forever to get anywhere.

CHAPTER SEVENTEEN

The sky was starting to show signs of light off in the east when Sam and Helen first saw the flicker of light from a distant campfire. The fire was back in among some cottonwood trees in a shallow draw making it hard to see. Several of the riders spotted the fire first and raced on ahead while Sam picked his way around some shallow gullies in the early morning dawn.

Helen strained to see where Casey might be, but she could not see him. She could barely see the riders in the predawn light, let alone a man lying on the ground.

As they grew closer to the fire, Sam and Helen could see the men gathered around what looked like a bedroll on the ground near the fire, but they were still unable to see Casey. Sam drove the wagon into the camp and up close to the fire. The men stepped away to reveal Casey lying on a bedroll with a blanket over him.

Anger immediately swelled up in Sam at the sight of his foreman and friend lying injured on the ground, but he had to control his temper if he was going to help him. It would do Casey no good for him to be so anger he could not help him.

"Get back, please," Helen said to those gathered around Casey as she jumped down from the wagon.

The men stepped back giving Helen room to get by. She went right to Casey's side and knelt down beside him. All she could see was the blood all over his face. She lifted the blanket covering him. As she quickly looked him over, she could see his clothes were torn in several places. She could also see there were small amounts of blood over most of his chest and stomach. As Helen examined him for other injuries, she discovered Casey's leg was twisted in a way that was not normal.

"Casey, can you hear me?" Helen asked softly as she leaned close to him.

"Yes, Ma'am," he replied, his voice weak and strained from the pain in his body.

"You'll be all right."

Casey slowly opened his eyes and looked up at her. To him she had the face of an angel. He smiled as best he could, then slowly closed his eyes again.

"Sam, help me," Helen said as she turned and looked up at him.

Sam knelt down beside his friend and looked at Helen. He had seen this done to a man only once before. He seriously doubted Helen had ever seen it. As he looked back down at Casey, he silently swore to himself that the men who did this would pay dearly for it.

"Help me get his shirt off," Helen said as she started to unbutton Casey's shirt.

Helen pulled his shirt open and saw all the tiny puncture wounds on his chest, arms and stomach. It set her back on her heels, and she gasped at the sight.

"My God, what happened to him?"

"He was wrapped in barbed wire, then they dragged him," Sam replied angrily.

"What? Who would do such a thing to another person?" Helen asked as she came to grips with what she had to do.

"I don't know, but I WILL find out," Sam replied as he tried to control his growing anger.

"Help me get his clothes off. We'll need to put him on a clean blanket and get him back to the house as quickly as possible."

Sam and Jacob helped her get Casey's clothes off while two of the other men took their knives and cut the boot off Casey's twisted leg. Helen quickly covered him with a clean sheet and blanket before he could catch a chill in the cool morning air.

"We need to move him to the wagon, but we have to straighten his leg first," she said as she looked at Sam.

Sam looked at her and wondered if she knew what she was doing. Since she had jumped right in and started treating Casey's wounds, he quickly decided she knew what to do. He immediately started giving instructions to his men.

"Jacob, get me a couple of long straight branches. We'll splint his leg."

Jacob began looking for the branches. Bill joined in to help. They were able to find a few fairly straight branches among the cottonwood trees that grew in the bottom of the gully. It was only a few minutes before they had gathered together what was needed to make a splint.

"Casey, this is going to hurt. Your leg is broken. We are going to have to set it. Do you understand?" Sam asked.

"I understand," Casey whispered as he opened his eyes and looked up at Helen. "It would be nice if that pretty little angel would let me hold her hand."

Helen smiled down at him and reached out her hand to him. She took Casey's hand in hers, then looked at Sam and nodded.

"I'm ready," Casey whispered as he looked up at Helen.

Sam moved down to Casey's feet and took hold of his foot. He looked up at Casey to make sure he was ready. Sam gritted his teeth and pulled as he straightened Casey's leg. Casey cried out in pain, then slumped into unconsciousness.

Helen felt his grip loosen on her hand, but she held onto him. She reached out with her free hand

and touched Casey's chest to make sure he was still alive. It was a relief to find he had simply lost consciousness. He was still breathing.

Sam looked at Helen for some kind of assurance Casey was still with them. When Helen indicated he had simply passed out, Sam pulled on his leg again. The bone sort of snapped back in place.

"Okay, get the splint on him while I hold his leg," Sam said as he looked at Jacob.

Jacob quickly began to put the splint on Casey's leg. He tied the two branches, one on either side of Casey's leg, with several leather straps to hold it firmly in place. When he was finished, Sam carefully laid Casey's leg back down on the ground.

By this time the sun was up and a golden glow began to cover the land under the bright sun. It was starting to warm up a little as well.

Casey was resting peacefully in a semi-conscious state. He would mumble from time to time, but it was nothing anyone could understand. The changing expressions on his face indicated he was going in and out of pain.

The next thing that had to be done was to move him to the wagon so he could be taken back to the ranch house where his wounds could be cleaned and dressed. At Sam's instructions, the men gathered around Casey, three on each side. They took hold of the blanket Casey was resting on then all together they carefully lifted him up off the ground and carried him to the wagon. They gently laid him down on the bed of blankets in the bottom of the wagon.

Helen got into the wagon and knelt down beside Casey's head. She carefully lifted his head and gently placed it in her lap, then looked toward Sam. She nodded she was ready.

"Davy and Bill, tie your horses to the back of the wagon and take the wagon back to the house. Go slow and make Casey's ride as smooth as you can. When you get there, help Helen in any way you can. And keep your eyes open."

"What are you going to do?" Helen asked.

"I'm going to try to find out who did this to him."

Helen could see by the determined look on Sam's face he was going to find who had done this and make them pay for it, and the sooner the better. She didn't want him to go, but she knew there was no way she would be able to stop him. It was something that had to be done. The men who did this to Casey had shown they would do anything to get what they wanted. Unless it was stopped, there would be more injuries or killings of Sam's ranch hands.

"Get moving and be careful," Sam ordered Davy who was now sitting on the seat of the wagon.

Davy started the team of horses back across the prairie toward the ranch house. Helen sat in the back of the wagon with Casey and watched Sam as they slowly moved away.

As soon as the wagon was out of sight, Sam turned to the men who were still with him.

"I want to know how Casey got left alone," he demanded. "I gave orders that no one was to be alone out here."

The men who had ridden out with Casey stood there looking at each other. All of them were feeling guilty about leaving Casey alone. It took a minute or two before one of them spoke up.

"We found Mr. Carter's cattle just like Casey said we would. He told us to gather them up while he checked the fence. When we got back to where we had left him, he wasn't there. We drove the cattle back through the fence then started looking for him. We found him here all wrapped in barbed wire," Jacob said."

"Why did you leave him alone?" Sam asked with a discussed tone in his voice.

"We did what he told us to do. Davy told him we wasn't supposed to split up, but he insisted we get the cattle," Joe said.

"As soon as we found him, we cut the barbed wire off him and sent Jess for you," Jacob added.

Although Sam was angry that they had left Casey alone, he knew the men respected Casey. Casey was the one they were used to taking orders from. As far as they were concerned, Casey was the boss when Sam was not around. Sam also realized it was too late to blame anyone. It would not make any difference now.

"Well, what's done is done. There isn't anything we can do to change it."

"What you plannin' on doin', boss?" Joe asked.

"We're going to find out who did this to Casey and turn them over to the law," Sam said.

"You mean to Sheriff Becker? That won't do no good," Joe objected, knowing full well what Becker thought of Sam.

"No, we're not going to turn them over to Becker. We're going to turn them over to the Territorial Marshal."

Sam watched as the men stood around looking at one another. They didn't know Sam had sent for Marshal Franklin.

"Have you sent for him already?" Joe asked.

"Yes. I sent a letter to him yesterday morning."

"It will take a spell for him to get here," Joe said.

"Yes, it will. In the meantime, we'll take care of our own."

The men had heard of Marshal Franklin. They knew him to be a good honest lawman. They all seemed to approve of him coming here.

"It's time to get moving. Break camp and get mounted up."

Sam started walking around the campsite looking at the ground. He was looking for tracks he hoped would lead him to the men responsible for his foreman's injuries. It wasn't long before Sam found signs in the dirt showing where Casey had been dragged across the ground. There were tracks from about six, maybe seven horses. Sam noticed one of the horses had a grove cut in his left front horseshoe. He was sure the identifying mark in the horseshoe would help him identify at least one of the cowards who attacked Casey.

Sam walked along the marks in the ground made by Casey when they dragged him. He followed them until he came to where the hole in the fence had been. There, he knelt down on the ground and examined the tracks again. He found something there he had not expected to find.

There were at least six sets of boot prints in the dirt, but one of them caught his attention. One of the boot prints showed there was some kind of a metal plate on the right heel, and that the boot prints were deeper on one side. That would indicate whoever wore those boots didn't walk straight and probably had a limp.

Sam stood up and looked across the fence to where the tracks had come from. He then turned around to see six of his ranch hands sitting on their horses watching and waiting for instructions.

He turned back around and could see the tracks in the dry grass moved out into the pasture on Carter's side of the fence. They then turned slightly and moved parallel to the fence line. Sam again had to wonder if some of Carter's line riders carried out the attack on Casey. There was also the possibility that Carter had hired some gunmen to set a trap for his men when they came to fix the fence.

Sam had heard rumors that a couple of Carter's ranch hands had rather questionable backgrounds. Since Carter had fought for the Confederacy during the war, it was not hard for him to believe the rumor that at least two of Carter's ranch hands were former confederate soldiers that had once ridden with Quantrail. Quantrail's Raiders, as they were called, was one of the last groups of renegade Confederate soldiers making their living by raiding farms and ranches in some of the so called 'Border States'.

There was no doubt in Sam's mind Carter had his men cut the fence so his cattle could get water from Sam's watering holes. There was also no doubt they would expect Sam's men to come along and fix the fence. It would be logical to think Sam would put more line riders out to prevent it from happening again. If that was the case, Sam was convinced Carter's men had set a trap for whoever came to fix the fence.

Sam turned back around and looked at his men again. He saw Joe was holding the reins of Casey's horse. Sam walked up to Joe and took the reins of the horse. He put his foot in the stirrup and swung up into the saddle.

"I'm going to follow those tracks to the end. Any of you who are not up to this can go back to the ranch house with nothing said. You were not hired for this."

Sam watched as the men checked their guns and sat up a little straighter in their saddles. They were ready to follow him into hell, if necessary. All the men liked Casey, and had a great deal of respect for Sam. They had no respect for anyone who would wrap a man up in barbed wire and then drag him through the dirt.

"We're ready, boss," Jack said.

Sam nodded his approval of his men for their courage then gave the order.

"Cut the fence open."

Two of his ranch hands cut open the fence they had closed just hours ago. Sam reined his horse around and rode him through the hole in the fence. Stopping just inside of Carter's property, Sam reined up and waited for the others to join him.

Once they were all on Carter's side of the fence, Sam instructed a couple of his hands to close the hole in the fence again. He knew it was going to put him on Carter's property with no easy way to get back to his own. Sam was determined to follow the tracks even if it took him right to Will Carter's front door.

As soon as the fence was repaired and his men were ready, Sam turned his horse and began to gallop along the trail left in the dried grass. It was easy to follow because that many horses tended to trample the short brittle grass down.

As they rode, Sam began to realize the trail they were following was drifting off away from where Carter's ranch house was located. If Carter had known about the hole in the fence or had put the hole in the fence, he was returning to his ranch house in a round about way. Sam had to wonder if maybe Carter's men were trying to make it look like Carter had nothing to do with what had happened to Casey.

After they had followed the trail for some distance, they came across a place where six men had camped for the night. They knew no one could follow them until morning. They had set up a dry camp, one without a fire, making it easier for them to get some rest without being discovered.

Sam was beginning to wonder what was going on. The trail left for him to follow was a little too obvious. It occurred to him that the trail might have been left for the soul purpose of setting him and his men up for a fight. If that was the case, Sam was ready and so were his men.

CHAPTER EIGHTEEN

The longer Sam and his men rode, the closer they got to the road into Shallow Creek or out of Elkhorn Valley, depending on which way they went. But either way, the trail was taking them further away from Will Carter's ranch house, which confused Sam.

Sam had convinced himself that Will Carter or his men were responsible for Casey's injuries. The fact that the riders didn't seem to be covering their trail at all, made Sam think he and his men might be riding into a trap. He had to wonder where the men they had been chasing were going.

Sam had to consider the fact that those who had injured Casey didn't seem to be headed for Will Carter's ranch house. If Carter had nothing to do with the attack on Casey, there was always the possibility some of Carter's men had taken things into their own hands to escalate the problems in order to cause a range war.

It didn't matter to Sam if Carter ordered the attack on Casey or not. As far as he was concerned, Will Carter was still responsible for the actions of his men regardless of who gave the orders.

It wasn't long before Sam and his men came to a gate in the fence. The trail made it clear the riders had gone through the gate. Sam reached down from the saddle and opened the gate that would let them off Will Carter's land and out onto the road. When they got to the road, Sam stopped and closed the gate. He then took a minute to check for the tracks in the dirt to see which way they went.

"Looks like they're headin' for town," Jack said.

"Yeah, it sure does. Do we follow them?" Sam asked as he looked at his men.

"We're with you, boss," Jack said with a note of confidence.

"Okay. We'll follow them to town, but we will not cause any trouble. We don't want to be the ones starting a range war. Can I count on all of you?" Sam asked as he sat in his saddle and looked at each of his men for a response.

"I can't speak for the others, but I'm ready for a fight," Jess said. "But I won't start it, boss."

The rest of his men quickly agreed. All the men seemed ready for a fight, but Sam was a little worried as to whether a fight with Carter's men would be a fair one. He had no idea who these men were they were following. They could be ranch hands, like his men, or they could be hired guns, professional killers. Sam tended to lean toward them being hired killers if for no other reason than to be better prepared for the worst.

"Okay. We ride to town together and we stay together. No one starts anything. If, and I say 'IF', a fight erupts you can defend yourself and each other. Agreed?"

"Agreed," Joe replied after looking around to see if there was anyone who might not agree.

Sam nodded then turned his horse toward town. His men fell in behind on the road toward the town of Shallow Creek. Like a small troop of soldiers, they rode at an easy gallop along the dusty road. Each member of the small band of ranch hands was wondering what the day would bring, but each of them was ready to fight for the brand and for Casey, if necessary.

Sam continued to watch the tracks left by the horses they had followed off of Will Carter's Ranch. There was little doubt in Sam's mind they were headed for town. All Sam could think about was that those who had attacked Casey were on their way to celebrate the deed they had done. That thought made Sam mad.

The more time Sam had to think about what had happened to Casey, and what had been happening over the past few days, the more he began to wonder if this latest incident might indeed be a trap. If those who had wrapped Casey in barbed wire last night had not wanted anyone to know who did it, they would not have left a trail that was so easy to follow. Or would they? They might if they thought it would point the blame toward someone else, like Will Carter, for example.

Sam began to wonder what it was they were riding into. They could be riding into hell for all he knew. He also began to think of ways to find out before it was too late.

As Sam and his men approached the town of Shallow Creek, Sam raised his arm in the air and stopped. His men stopped and gathered around him in the middle of the road.

"I've got a feeling this might be a trap," Sam said as he looked at his men. "The trail has been way too easy to follow."

"You think they're waitin' for us to ride inta town?" Jack asked.

Sam paused for a moment before he answered. "I have to think that. I think they want us to ride right down the middle of the street making us sitting ducks.

"When I got shot in town," Sam continued. "The two that tried to bushwhack me tried to get me in a crossfire in the middle of the street."

"You think they're plannin' on tryin' it again?" Jess asked.

"Yes. I think that's a very good possibility," Sam replied.

Sam could see by the look on the faces of some of the men that they were thinking over what he had said.

"That's good enough for me. What do you think we should do about it?" Jacob asked.

"Jacob, you were a scout during the war, weren't you?"

"Yes, sir. But I fought for the south," he replied with a note of pride in his voice.

"That doesn't matter any more. We're fighting together now. I want you to sneak into town, or at least as close as you can get without being seen. Find out as much as you can about what's going on. We'll hold up over there among those trees and behind those rocks. We'll be waiting for you."

"Yes, sir," Jacob said, then reined his horse around and started toward town at a gallop.

Sam motioned for the rest of the ranch hands to move around behind the rocks and to keep quiet. Just before he turned his horse to join his ranch hands, he took a look in the direction Jacob had gone.

Jacob rode on toward town until he came close to the outskirts of Shallow Creek. He turned his horse off the road into a small grove of trees.

After tying his horse to a tree, he began working his way along a shallow gully. The gully ran along the side of the road close to the town before it turned and wandered around behind the town's buildings. He had fairly good cover provided by the old cottonwood trees in and along the edge of the gully.

At the edge of town, Jacob squatted down behind some bushes where the gully turned. He could see down most of the street. At first he didn't see anything out of the ordinary, but then he caught some movement out of the corner of his eye.

He turned and watched where he thought he had seen something move, but couldn't see anything. As he continued to watch, he saw movement again. This time it became all too clear what it was he was seeing. There was someone on the roof of the jail.

What he had seen was a man moving around on the roof. The man had apparently become impatient. He stood up and moved to the front of the building. He looked across the street toward the saloon as if he wished he could be there instead of on a hot roof. By simply moving around, the man had given away his position.

Jacob immediately began looking for others on the roofs of the other buildings. He saw the head of another man pop up then quickly duck back down behind the sign on the roof of the Red Garter Saloon. It quickly became clear that Sam had been right. They were planning to ambush Sam and his men when they came into town. They were going to bushwhack them right in front of the jail.

Jacob turned his attention back to the street. He noticed there was only a couple of horses and a freight wagon on the street. From the looks of the horse dung behind the horses at the hitching rails, they had been there for some time. He didn't think the men they had been following would have been in town very long. It made him wonder where the men had left their horses.

Jacob moved along the shallow gully until he came to a place where he could see down along behind some of the buildings on one side of Shallow Creek. There in back of the saloon were six horses, all of them saddled and ready to ride. Jacob smiled to himself. He was sure he had found where the leaders were. He took a few minutes to assess the situation.

Jacob could see there was not a great deal of cover for Sam and his men to come in from behind the buildings. There were very few trees close to town and very little other cover such as bushes. However, there was the large storage shed behind the Red Garter Saloon that Jake used to store supplies. It would provide some cover, but it would be very difficult to get to the shed without being seen.

Jacob looked over the area and examined it for ways to sneak into town. The only way to get to the back of the saloon was to go down along the dried creek bed and come up behind the Red Garter Saloon using the shed for cover. The only problem was they would be in the open for a good fifty feet or more. If they were seen while they moved from the gully to behind the shed, the element of surprise would be lost.

It appeared it would be easier to get behind the jail without being seen. There was a small ridge with brush over it a man could use for cover. The ridge ran the full length of the town.

As soon as Jacob was sure he had all the information on the trap he could get without being seen, he snuck back to his horse. Then he returned to where Sam and the other ranch hands were waiting.

Sam listened very carefully to what Jacob had to say. It didn't look good. At least they were fairly evenly matched as far as numbers went.

Sam sat on the ground with Jacob and Jack while the others looked on. They were discussing the few options they had.

"As best as I can figure it, there are two men on the roofs and four in the saloon," Jacob explained.

"Maybe five in the saloon," Sam said.

"Five?" Jack asked, wondering where Sam came up with the extra man.

"The sheriff. My guess would be he will be in on this. He's either in the saloon with the others, or he is in the jail where he can back up those in the saloon. There's always the possibility he will stay out of it all together if things start to go bad for them. But we can't count on that," Sam said.

"You might be right," Jacob replied. "I didn't see him around."

"He might have left town so he ain't a part of this. You know, so he can't be ta blame for it," Jack said.

"You could be right, but we can't count on that. Here's my plan," Sam said as he interrupted the speculation on where Sheriff Becker might be.

"Jacob, you will work your way around behind the saloon. You should be able to get up on the roof at the back corner of the saloon. I want you to take out the one on the roof of the saloon and cover the backdoor of the saloon until we get there. The roof of the saloon is higher than the roof of the jail. With the high store front you should be able to do it without the one on the roof of the jail seeing you."

"Jack, I want you and Slim to work your way along the brush covered ridge to behind the jail. When you get to the jail, I want one of you to take out the guy on the roof while the other one goes into the jail through the backdoor to make sure it's clear. Do it at the same time so there's no warning. Disarm anyone you find and put them in a cell."

"Does that include Becker?"

"Yes. I want this done as quickly and quietly as possible," Sam replied flatly.

"Got it. What are you going to do?" Jacob asked.

"The rest of us will ride into town and cut in between the freight office and the building on this side of it. We will work our way to the front of the saloon on foot. I'm counting on you to keep the back of the saloon covered until we can get into position."

"Sounds like a good plan," Jacob agreed.

"Just be careful who you shoot at. I don't want you to shoot at anyone unless you have to. When the shooting starts, be sure of who you are shooting at. Got it?" Sam said.

"We got it, boss," Jack said.

"Let's get at it. We'll give you guys a five-minute head start. By the way, I want as many of them alive as we can get, but don't risk your own life for it."

Jacob nodded that he understood as did Jack and Slim. Sam watched them as they walked over to their horses. Sam checked his pocket watch. He was to give them a head start, but he didn't want them left out there for very long without anyone to help them.

As soon as Jacob, Jack and Slim were out of sight, Sam stood up and walked over to his horse. He mounted up and watched as the rest of the ranch hands took their cue from him and did the same.

Sitting on top of his horse, he took time to check his guns and to make sure the rest of his ranch hands were ready for what was to come. As he levered a cartridge into the chamber of his Winchester, he looked over the faces of the two who were going in with him. There was no doubt in his mind they were nervous, maybe even a little frightened.

It was normal for the men to be nervous before going into battle. He was sure several of them who had served during the Civil War could remember what it was like before a battle. They were more than likely feeling that way right now.

After a glance at his pocket watch, Sam knew it was time to move out. He took another brief look at his men. They were as ready as they were every going to be.

"Okay, let's move out," he said.

Sam walked his horse out onto the road and started toward town. His men quickly joined him on the road. They moved closer to Shallow Creek at a walk in sort of a ragged single file down the road.

The air was dry, as were the mouths of the riders. There was no breeze to cut the heat of the day. The dust of the road swirled around the hooves of the horses as they slowly moved toward town. Each one of them was nervously looking around, trying to spot danger before it had a chance to catch them by surprise.

As they approached the edge of town, Sam could see Jack on the roof of the jail and Jacob on the roof of the saloon. They were waving their arms to let him know they had taken out the men on the roofs.

Sam and the rest of the ranch hands rode slowly along the side of the street the saloon was on in the hope of not being seen before they were ready. When they got to the freight station, they turned in along side the building and jumped off their horses and let them go.

Sam leaned up against the building with his rifle held tightly in his hand. He looked across the street to make sure Jack was where he was supposed to be. Jack waved down at Sam then took up his position behind the false front of the Sheriff's Office.

"Jess, you go to the back corner of the building and keep watch down along behind the building. Jacob may need help. If they bust out the back of the saloon, do what you can to keep them from getting to their horses," Sam said.

The young man nodded and quickly moved to the back corner of the building. As soon as Sam was sure he was ready and in position, he motioned for Joe to follow him.

Sam looked around the corner. He was covered from above the Saloon and the jail, but he was not sure if anyone was inside any of the other buildings across the street.

Sam and Joe quickly moved around in front of the freight station, using the wagon and the large freight boxes for cover. He kept a close eye on the front of the saloon. Sam wanted no surprises.

In the area between the saloon and the freight office there was a narrow alley. In order for Sam to position himself in front of the saloon he would have to cross the alley. He would have no cover from anyone who might be in one of the buildings across the street. He would be exposed to anyone who might be there.

So far all had gone well, almost too well. There was no indication anything had gone wrong, or that the men in the saloon had any idea Sam and his men had arrived in town. Sam knew the element of surprise could be lost at any moment. And when that happened, all hell would break loose.

CHAPTER NINETEEN

The time to press on and trap the others in the saloon had come. Sam was hopeful the arrests could be made without much of a fight, but there was a slim chance of that happening.

Sam could hear a little of what was going on in the saloon. He could hear voices, but could not make out very much of what was being said. It seemed there were at least two who were doing a lot of bragging and doing it rather loudly. From what Sam could piece together, it was about wrapping Casey in barbed wire which confirmed what he believed.

It seemed to Sam that he and his men had been in town for a long time when in fact it had only been a few minutes. Sam found it hard to believe that the men they were after had not heard or seen them. They were apparently celebrating too much to realize Sam and his men were already there.

The only reason Sam could think of for them being so casual about what they had done was they didn't expect Sam to be in town so soon. The more Sam heard them celebrate, the angrier he became. Sam wanted revenge more than he wanted justice.

Suddenly, Sam's attention was drawn to the creaking sound of the swinging doors of the saloon as they swung open. One of the men started out of the saloon, but stopped. Sam ducked behind a large wooden box, resting his rifle over the top. He could hear someone call out to the man who started out of the saloon.

"Looks like they ain't inta no fight today," someone inside called out, a hint of laughter could be heard in his voice.

"I guess not," the one at the door said as he looked back inside the saloon and laughed.

"Maybe they need more time to work up the guts to come after us," he added with a chuckle.

The man who was about to step out of the saloon had a big grin on his face. He stepped out away from the door and turned as if he was planning to go on across the street.

He stopped suddenly. The grin slowly disappeared from his face and his mouth fell open when he saw Sam and Joe on the porch of the freight station with their rifles aimed directly at him. His eyes got big and he started to slowly take a step backward. His eyes were filled with fear. He knew he was about to die.

"They're here," the man yelled out as he grabbed for his six-gun, but he was too late and way too slow.

Sam pulled the trigger on his rifle. The loud crack of his gun let everyone know the fight was on. The bullet from Sam's rifle caught the man in his side just below his ribs as he tried to duck back inside the saloon. The force of the bullet spun the man around as it slammed him back against the edge of the door. He bounced off the doorway, spun around and began to fall. As he fell, he stumbled over a chair and then rolled off the boardwalk into the street. He lay bleeding in the dirt between the boardwalk and a hitching rail. There was no doubt he was out of the fight.

All at once the air was filled with the sounds of gunfire and the smell of gun smoke. There was also the sound of glass breaking and wood splitting as bullets crashed through the windows and ripped through the window frames in the front of the saloon.

The shooting didn't last for more then a minute or two. As quickly as the shooting had started, it was quiet again. Sam leaned against the large box as he reloaded his gun. He had no idea if anyone had even been hit, other than the one lying in the street. He felt someone had to have been hit with all the lead flying around.

Sam's attention was quickly drawn to the sound of a thud just a few feet in front of him. He looked around the corner of the box and saw a pistol lying in the dirt between the buildings.

Sam looked up to see Jacob standing on the roof of the saloon looking down at him. Lying at Jacob's feet was the limp body of the man who had been on the roof. Jacob gave Sam a sign that all was well. It was a relief for Sam to know Jacob and Jack were all right. The only ones he didn't know about were Slim who had gone with Jack to take control of the jail, and Jess who was watching the back of the saloon.

"You want to give it up in there and come out?" Sam called out.

"You kidding, mister," a husky voice replied.

"The choice is yours. You can come out and go to jail, or you can be carried out. Frankly, I don't care which you choose," Sam said forcefully.

"I guess you're going to have to come in and get us. You might remember we've got a friend of yours in here."

Sam looked around. He was sure they didn't have any of his ranch hands. They were all accounted for except for Slim who was supposed to be at the jail. That left only one other person Sam could think of and that was his friend, Jake.

"Jake, you okay?" Sam called out.

"Yeah, so far," he called back.

"But he ain't goin' to be for very long if you don't back off and let us go."

Sam leaned back against the building to think. He had three men trapped in the saloon, but they had his friend. There was nowhere for them to go. The only problem was Jake. He didn't want anything to happen to Jake, but he didn't want these men getting away, either.

Sam didn't know who these men were he had trapped in the saloon, but he had known men like them. They were ruthless and unpredictable. They would do anything, even kill one of their own, if it meant the difference between getting away or getting captured. Sam was convinced they would kill Jake even if he let them go. He was not about to let it happen if he could prevent it.

Suddenly there were a couple of shots from the back corner of the freight station. They were followed by the sounds of horses running away.

Sam looked up at Jacob and motioned for him to see what was going on behind the saloon. He watched as Jacob stepped over the dead man on the roof and quickly scampered to the back of the saloon.

When Jacob got to the back of the saloon, he saw the horses running off across the prairie. None of them had riders. It looked as if they had been run off. He took a moment to look over the edge of the saloon. He saw one of the men they were after holding his arm as he lay on the ground. He was not dead, but he was in a great deal of pain. There was no doubt that he was out of the fight, and he would not be going anywhere real soon.

Jacob looked down behind the freight station and saw Jess lying behind a box with his rifle across the top of the box. He had run the horses off and shot the man lying in the dirt. Jacob signaled his approval and moved back to the front of the saloon.

"Jess ran off their horses and shot one of them," Jacob said just loud enough for Sam to hear.

Sam nodded that he understood. It gave him an idea. Jacob had one dead man on the roof. Jack had at least one man over at the jail, although Sam wasn't sure if the one Jack had was in jail or if he was dead. All he knew for sure was Jack had moved into the jailhouse to cover the front door of the saloon.

"I don't know who you are, but I will tell you this," Sam called out. "You will not get out of here alive if you don't surrender. You kill my friend and I will personally hang you on the big cottonwood at the south end of town and let the buzzards pick your bones clean. And I can assure you it will be a long slow death."

"You talk tough, but you ain't got what it takes," the husky voice replied, then laughed.

"I don't? Well, we'll see," Sam called back.

Looking up at Jacob, he whispered. "When I signal you, I want you to shoot, scream and then toss that body down right in front of the saloon doors."

Jacob smiled as he began to grasp what Sam had in mind then picked up the body. He carried the dead man to a place on the roof directly above the front doors of the saloon. He held the body up in front of him, then turned and waited for Sam's signal.

"I've got a couple of your men. Just to show you I mean business, I'm going to kill one of them," Sam yelled so he was sure the man in the saloon heard him and there was no misunderstanding as to what Sam meant.

"You don't have the nerve," the man inside said defiantly, his voice showing a bit of laughter to it.

"I don't?"

Sam didn't wait for a response from the man inside. He had Jacob fire his gun, scream and then toss the already dead man off the roof. The body landed with a thud on the boardwalk right in front of the saloon doors where it could be seen from inside.

Sam didn't say anything, he simple waited for a response from the man inside. It seemed like it took forever for anyone to say anything.

"You son of a . . ," the man inside said, the shock of what he saw causing him to choke on his own words.

"There were six of you when you tied my foreman up with barbed wire and drug him. Now there is only two of you left in there. Your horses are gone and I'm about ready to kill the one you had waiting for us on the jailhouse roof if you don't throw down your guns and come out with your hands in the air. You've got one minute to decide,"

Sam said with all the authority in his voice he could muster.

Sam waited and watched the front door of the saloon. He pulled his pocket watch out and looked at it as the thin second hand move around the face of it ticking off the seconds.

Sam didn't know if they would give up, or if they would make it a fight to the finish. Only time would tell and it was passing by at a snail's pace.

"You've got thirty seconds," Sam called out, but there was no response.

Sam took this silent time to look around. Jack was across the street in the jailhouse, his gun pointing out the window. Jacob was on the roof of the saloon watching the front of the saloon from up above. Joe was beside him, waiting to see what was going to happen next, but ready for anything. And Jess was watching the back of the saloon. All was well, or was it.

Sam remembered he was short one ranch hand. Where was Slim? He had gone with Jack around behind the jailhouse, but where was he now? Sam quickly realized he would have to worry about Slim later. Right now he had other things to do.

"Times up," Sam called out. "Jack, get the man you have and bring him to the front door of the jail."

Sam waited. He wasn't sure if this was going to work or not, but he had to try everything he could to get them to surrender.

It took a little while, but finally the door of the jailhouse slowly started to open. Gradually a man appeared at the door. He had a rope tied around his neck and his hands were tied behind his back. The expression on his face was one of pure terror. The man knew he was about to die.

Sam's heart sank. It was hard for Sam to believe the man Jack had captured was hardly more than a kid. Sam thought about calling off his bluff, but to do that would mean Jake might not survive the day. The young man had set his course, now he was going to have to live or die with the consequences of his choice.

"You've got one minute to toss your guns out and come out with your hands in the air, or I will have him killed," Sam called out.

Jack, staying out of sight behind the door just inside the jail, raised his gun up and put it to the kid's head. It was in plain sight to those in the saloon. There was no mistaking what was about to happen.

"Oh, please don't let 'um kill me," the young man cried out.

"You've got thirty seconds," Sam called out.

Jack pulled back the hammer of his pistol. The sound of the gun cocking rang in the young man's ear like a church bell.

"Please, Bart. Oh, God," the young man cried.

Again there was what seemed like a long period of silence before anything happened. The tension in the air was as thick as the fog along a river on an early spring morning.

"Okay, you win," Bart called back from inside the saloon.

"Throw out your guns," Sam demanded.

Several pistols and a couple rifles came flying out the front door of the saloon and landed in the dirt of the street.

"Okay, come out with your hands up," Sam ordered.

Sam motioned for Jack to take his prisoner back inside the jail. As soon as he saw the young man pulled back into the jailhouse, he readied himself for anything. He was not sure if Bart was going to try something, or if he would go to jail peacefully. He signaled Jacob to cover them.

Bart came out of the saloon with his hands up in the air. He had a potbelly and long dirty hair and beard. His hands were big, and from the look of him, he was big enough to take on a grizzly bear.

"Move out to the center of the street," Sam ordered.

The big man did as he was told. Although Bart knew he was captured, his eyes dared anyone to give him the slightest chance and he would kill them. Sam was not going to give him the chance.

"Jake, anyone else left in there?" Sam called out.

"Just the body of one of these animals," Jake said as he walked out of the saloon into the sunlight. "He got his in the first round of gunfire."

"Any idea as to who it is?"

"No. I never saw any of 'um before."

"Are you okay?" Sam asked as he watched Jake turn around and look at the front of his saloon.

"Yeah, I'm fine, but will you look at my saloon. It's all shot up. It'll take me two months to get new glass and put it back the way it was."

"We can work something out, but first I've got to get this one to jail."

Jess and Joe, along with Sam escorted Bart to the jailhouse. As Sam followed along behind, he noticed the boot print Bart left in the dirt of the street. It was the same as the one he had found where Casey had been attacked. These were the men he was after.

As soon as Bart was safely locked up in the jail, Sam sat down at the desk in the jail. He was trying to decide what to do next when Slim came hobbling in the backdoor of the jailhouse. Everyone looked at him, wondering where he had been.

"What happened to you?" Sam asked.

"I stepped in a prairie dog hole and twisted my ankle," he replied with a slight hint of embarrassment.

"We'll get Doc over here to take a look at it. Joe, go get the doctor."

"Boss, we goin' to keep 'um locked up here?" Jacob asked.

"Yeah. You got a better idea?"

"No, sir. What's goin' to happen when the sheriff gets back? Is he goin' to let them loose?"

"Not if I can help it."

"Say, Jake. Where is our sheriff?"

"I don't know. He left town this morning right after these fellas showed up."

"I'm not surprised. Get the guy from behind the saloon and the one in the street over here. We'll have Doc look at all of them," Sam said to his ranch hands.

CHAPTER TWENTY

Sam's men gathered up their prisoners and got them all locked securely in the jail. Joe returned with Doc Miller who immediately began taking care of the wounded. There was nothing Doc could do for the man who had been gut shot in front of the saloon other than to make him as comfortable as possible. He was too far gone and would most likely not last the night.

The one that Joe had shot behind the saloon would probably have very little use of his right arm for the rest of his life. He had been shot in the elbow smashing the joint. However, he would live long enough to hang with the others. The kid and Bart were relatively uninjured, while the remaining members of the gang were dead.

As soon as Doc Miller was finished taking care of the prisoners, Sam began questioning them. It quickly became apparent they had no intentions of telling him who had hired them, even under the threat of ending up on the short end of a rope, which was where they would end up anyway.

The one thing that seemed to be clear to Sam was Bart didn't seem the slightest bit nervous about hanging. It seemed strange to Sam. He thought Bart should have been at least a little nervous. It was not normal to see men, even tough men like Bart, so relaxed when he should know he stood a very good chance of ending up swinging from the gallows.

There was something about Bart's attitude that gave Sam the impression if he left them in jail, they wouldn't be there very long. That led Sam to think it might be best to lock up the sheriff along with them. Locking up Becker probably wouldn't go over very well with the Territorial Marshal when he arrived, unless there was some real good solid proof that he was involved with the others. At this point, Sam didn't have any proof.

While Doc Miller wrapped Slim's ankle, Sam moved over and sat down beside him.

"Doc, if we leave these men here, Becker is going to let them loose as soon as he gets back from hiding. Is there any chance you could get the town council to quickly elect a Town Marshal and put him in charge of keeping them in jail?"

"I think I might be able to get it done, but who would you suggest for the job? We've got mostly storekeepers here in town. They aren't going to want to be a Town Marshal and still try to keep their stores open. Besides, none of them know much about using a gun. Hell, half of them would probably shoot themselves in the foot if they tried to draw a gun in a hurry."

Sam rubbed his chin as he thought about what Doc had said. He knew Doc was probably right. Sam looked around the room as if looking for someone he felt could fill the job. As he looked at Jacob, he figured he might have found the right man for the job.

"I think I know just the man," Sam said. "He's as tough as they come, he can handle a gun as well, if not better than most men, and he is not afraid of anyone. He's also very savvy."

"If you know someone like that, I'd like to know who he is," Doc said.

"Jacob Henry."

Doc Miller looked over at Jacob and sort of nodded his head as he thought about Sam's suggestion. He didn't know Jacob very well, but what he knew about the man was good. He was convinced in his own mind Jacob was an honest man and knew how to handle himself. He was certainly a better man for the job than any of the town's men.

Jacob had been watching Doc and Sam talking, but he could hear only a few bits and pieces of their conversation. He wondered why Doc Miller was looking at him. It made him feel uneasy. It surprised him when Sam motioned for him to join them in their conversation.

"You want me, boss?" Jacob asked.

"What would you think of being the Town Marshal of Shallow Creek?" Sam asked.

Jacob looked from Sam to Doc Miller, then back to Sam. "I don't know anything about being a lawman," he said looking a bit confused.

"You don't have to know all that much. You're fair, you're honest, and you know what is right. You know how to use a gun when you have to, and you know when to just talk. What more do you need to know? You know how to read, that's more than some of the men around here. You can learn what the laws are with help from Doc and with some time spent studying a few law books. There are a couple of books about the law right here in this office," Sam said as he pointed to the law books on the desk.

Jacob looked down at the floor as he thought about what was being offered to him. He liked his job on the ranch. He had not planned to leave the ranch, but he knew this could prove to be a good opportunity for him.

"Are you trying to get rid of me, Boss?" Jacob asked.

"No, not at all, Jacob. You've been a good hand. I think you would make a good Marshal. This town needs a good, fair minded lawman."

"This town does need a fair minded lawman, that's for sure. But I wasn't planning on leaving the ranch."

"I know you weren't, but this town needs a good man like you to be the Town Marshal."

"I don't know," Jacob said, not sure of himself.

"I'll tell you what. You take the job as Town Marshal for a little while. If you don't like it and want to come back to the ranch, I'll keep a place for you. How's that?" Sam asked as he watched Jacob to get an idea of how he felt about the offer.

"That sounds fair, I guess," he replied after giving it some thought. "How much would I make as Marshal?"

"I'll see to it you get at least a few dollars more a month than you do as a ranch hand," Doc said with a smile.

"Okay," Jacob finally said after giving it some more thought. "Now don't you think your men can run wild in town just because I once worked for you," Jacob said to Sam with a smile.

"I won't," Sam replied with a slight chuckle. "I'm sure you'll treat them fair."

"I'll try. What do I have to do?" Jacob asked Doc.

"I'll get you approved by the town council, then we'll swear you in and get you a badge. Since the jail belongs to the town, not to the county, you can toss out anything belonging to Becker," Doc said. "In fact, you can move in right now. By the way, the town pays for your room and board at Ma Baker's boarding house. I'll tell her to expect you.

You board your horse at the livery stable at the town's expense, too."

"This is sounding better all the time. I'll take the job," Jacob said with a grin.

"Great, I'll be back in a few minutes," Doc said, then he stood and left the jailhouse.

"Boss, I take it you want me in this job?" Jacob asked as soon as Doc left.

"Yes, I do. I think you will make a good lawman. It's a good job and a good opportunity for you."

"What about Sheriff Becker? Won't he be pretty upset when he finds out I've taken his place here?"

"I suspect he will. He might even try to throw you out, but once you have the town's blessing, he'll have to find another place to set up his office."

"I understand. I also understand these are my prisoners. I'll keep them locked up until the judge comes by."

"I can leave you some help if you want," Sam offered.

"I can handle Becker, all right, but I would like a little help keeping watch over the prisoners."

"You've got it," Sam said.

"If Becker gives me any trouble, I'll put him in jail with the others."

"I don't think it'll be necessary, but you might have to do just that. Remember, you have no authority outside the town, but Doc Miller will explain your job to you when he gets back."

"That's good," Jacob said.

"We need to get back to the ranch and see how Casey is doing. Just so you know, if Casey dies, I'll want these men tried for murder."

"If Casey dies, they won't get out of jail until they're led off to hang," Jacob promised. "Casey's a good man and a good friend of mine."

"I'll leave Joe with you as your deputy. If the town won't pay for a deputy, I will. You'll need help guarding them so Becker doesn't let them out."

"Thanks, Boss."

Sam shook Jacob's hand and wished him well. He also reminded him that he could always come back to the ranch if he didn't like being a lawman.

With all the good-byes said from the rest of the ranch hands, they all started back for the ranch. It was a quiet ride for all of them. It had been a long day with their emotions running up and down like a horse on a carousel.

As the men rode into the ranch yard, Sam noticed there were still guards posted to keep an eye on things. Sam was sure very few of the chores had been done as most of his ranch hands had been with him or guarding the ranch. There was no doubt in his mind the rest of his ranch hands had not strayed very far from the ranch house, as they would be worried about Casey.

Sam rode up to the ranch house and got down off his horse. His men sat in their saddles waiting for orders and hoping to hear how Casey was doing. Sam turned and looked up at the ranch hands.

"Jack, I want you to take over as foreman until Casey is back on his feet. We have things to get done. This ranch won't run itself."

"Yes, sir. I think the men would like to know how Casey is doing before they get to work."

"I'll find out."

Sam knew how the men felt. He was as interested in finding out how Casey was doing as the rest.

As he turned around to go inside, Helen stepped out on the porch. Helen looked at Sam first, then looked up at the ranch hands. She didn't hesitate to tell them what she knew they wanted to know.

"Casey is doing fairly well right now. He's in a good deal of pain, but he is resting off and on. I think he will be all right, but it will take a while for him to recover."

"Thank you, Ma'am," Jack said as he reached up and touched the brim of his hat, then turned to the others. "Time to get to work."

The men turned around and rode off toward the barn. Sam watched as they left. He knew he had made a good choice in Jack to act as foreman in Casey's absence.

"How are you doing," Sam said as he stepped up on the porch next to Helen.

"I'm a little tired, but okay," she replied as she slipped her arm around behind him.

"I'd like to see Casey," Sam said as they walked into the house.

"He's resting right now, but you can look in on him."

Sam left Helen in the living room and went down the hall to the bedroom where Casey was. He looked in and saw his old friend lying on clean sheets. He had a lot of bandages on him, his leg was still splinted, and he was resting quietly. Sam let out a long sigh of relief knowing his foreman and long time friend was getting good care.

Sam quietly closed the bedroom door behind him and returned to the living room where Helen was waiting for him. He walked over to the sofa where Helen was sitting and sat down beside her. He leaned back, tipped his head back and closed his eyes.

After a few deep breaths, he opened his eyes and looked at Helen. He could see by the look in her eyes she wanted to know how things went and what happened, but she was patient about it. He would tell her in his own time and in his own way.

"I noticed you came back without Jacob and Joe. Are they all right?" Helen asked, a little worried about what might have happened to them.

"They're fine. Jacob has taken the job of Town Marshal and Joe is staying in town to be his deputy until our prisoners are tried."

"You caught them?"

"Yes, we did. We only had one injury in the process. Slim twisted his ankle when he stepped in a prairie dog hole."

Sam went on to tell her about what had happened. He made it a point to leave out some of the more gruesome details like when he had Jacob toss the body off the saloon roof. He thought it might not set well with her. Besides, he didn't feel it was necessary for her to know every little detail. The important thing was they had caught those who had injured Casey and they were going to stand trial for what they did.

"The only bad part is they won't talk and tell us who hired them," Sam said. "I sure would like to know."

"Since they came off Will Carter's ranch, do you think he might have hired them?"

"It sure looks that way, but I have my doubts. The one thing I can't get out of my mind is Frank Gregory has something to do with it. The problem is I don't know what."

"Do you feel that way because of the way he feels about you?" Helen asked.

"I suppose it could be, but I have a funny feeling about Carter. I don't think he would hire anyone to do his fighting for him. It doesn't add up. In fact, after I saw the condition of his cattle, I can't help but think he has already given up," Sam said.

"I would think he would have trouble getting enough money together to pay for men like Bart and his gang. Those kinds of men are not the kind to take on a job without some up front money."

"Then who do you think hired them?" Helen asked.

"My best guess would be Frank Gregory. He has some money, so I hear. He could hire the guns needed to do something like this. But you know, there's something else bothering me."

"What's that?" Helen asked, wanting to know everything on Sam's mind.

"The sharpshooter, the sniper that has been taking pot shots at us. Where does he fit into all this?"

"Maybe he's one of the men who injured Casey?"

"No, I don't think so. Most snipers are loners. They don't mix well with others and prefer it that way. They don't want to be seen or known. They want to do their job without fanfare. The men we captured wanted us to know they did it. They were waiting for us in town, and they fully expected to get us to ride right into their trap, right in the middle of town, where everyone could see."

"If what you're saying is right, then you could have two people after you."

"That's what I'm afraid of. The problem is I don't know who they are."

"It has been a long day and you're tired. Maybe if you got some rest things might look different in the morning," Helen suggested.

"What about you?"

"I've been able to get a little nap here and there while taking care of Casey. I will want to spend the night in the room with him in case he wakes up."

"Oh. I'll walk you to your room."

"Sure," she said with a smile.

Sam stood up and reached out to Helen. She took his hand and walked with him down the hall as far as the room Casey was in. They stopped, then Sam turned in front of her. He reached out, put his hands on her narrow waist and drew her up to him.

Helen reached up and put her arms around his neck and kissed him as she leaned against him. It was a gentle kiss meant to remind him that she cared about him.

Sam drew back, yawned and looked down at her. He smiled then said, "I think I better go get some sleep."

"I think you should, too. I'll see you in the morning."

With that said, Sam turned and walked on down the hall to his room.

As soon as Sam disappeared into his room, Helen turned and went into the room where Casey was resting. She checked to make sure he had not been moving around too much and opening his wounds. She then sat down in a big oversize chair she had been using to rest in. She pulled a large afghan up over herself and closed her eyes. It wasn't long before she was sleeping.

CHAPTER TWENTY-ONE

Helen slept all night in a chair beside the bed where Casey laid. Although she woke several times during the night to check on him, she rested well. Each time she checked on Casey, she found him sleeping quietly.

As the sun peeked in around the edges of the curtain covered window, Helen woke to find Casey still resting peacefully. He seemed to be breathing normally and didn't look as if he was in any pain at the moment. It pleased her to see that he seemed to be doing much better.

Helen stood up, folded the afghan and laid it over the back of the chair. She left the room as quietly as she could so as not to wake him. Helen went down the hall to the kitchen to get something to eat. While she was there she had hoped to see Sam, but he was not in the kitchen or in the dining room.

"Margaret, where is Sam?"

"He's gone," she replied.

"Where did he go?"

"I think he was going out to help move some cattle to another watering hole, but I'm not sure. With some of the men standing guard and some still in town, he needs to help the others with the chores.

He left right after breakfast, but he should be back soon, I think," Margaret explained.

Helen nodded she understood, but she was still disappointed she had missed seeing him. After getting something to eat, she went into the living room and walked over to the window. She drew the curtain back a little and looked out. All she could see were a few of the men doing their chores around the barn and a couple of the men standing guard. All was quiet at the moment.

As she was about to drop the curtain and return to her room to check on Casey, she saw Sam coming around the corner of the barn. Helen watched him as he rode his big black stallion into the ranch yard. She couldn't help but think how handsome he looked on a horse. He was tall with broad shoulders and strong arms. Arms she liked to have around her.

To her way of thinking, Sam sat a horse well. Even though his horse was big, Sam was tall enough to look good on it. He had the appearance of a man confident in what he was doing. He seemed to look the part of a ranch owner.

She dropped the curtain when she realized he was riding toward the house. Helen didn't want him to see her watching him. She felt it would be embarrassing for her.

Sam stepped down from his horse and tied him to the hitching rail. He then turned and stepped up on the porch. As he was about to reach for the door, he heard a voice call to him.

"Mr. Willard!"

Sam turned around to see one of his ranch hands coming toward him. He moved to the edge of the porch and waited for the ranch hand to come closer.

"Mr. Willard, we found another place in the fence that was cut, only this time it was the fence between your ranch and the Gregory Ranch."

"Really?" Sam asked, a little surprised they would find another cut in the fence so soon.

"Yes, sir. It was cut on purpose, too. From the looks of it, it was cut last night sometime."

"Any cattle run through it?"

"None as far as we could tell. We fixed the fence."

"Good. Did you happen to see anyone while you were out there?"

"Nope, not a soul."

"How many of you went out to check the fence line?"

"There was four of us, just like you ordered."

"Good. Thanks. If you see anything, you let me know."

"I will, sir."

Sam watched as the ranch hand turned and went back toward the barn. He wondered what was going on. The fence had been cut on the north side of his property and cattle run through it. Now it was cut on the south side with no sign of cattle at all. It struck Sam as strange. The only thing he could think of was that someone was trying to make it look as if Frank and Will were in it together, which was certainly a possibility. After all, it was common knowledge they were friends.

There was another possibility for the cut fence. It was possible someone had simply cut the fence in order to either come onto the Willard Ranch or to leave it. One of the shooters might have had to cut it a day or two ago after taking a shot at him or his men. It would be hard to tell if the fence was cut last night or several days ago. The weather had been too dry to cause the cut to show signs of rust in such a short time.

Sam turned back around and went inside the ranch house. As he stepped into the living room, he saw Helen looking at him. A smile quickly came over his face.

"I missed you at breakfast this morning," he said.

"I guess I was tired."

"I'm sure you were. How is Casey doing?"

"I think he will be all right, but it will be some time before he will be able to work."

"I'm sure. How are you doing?" Sam asked, his concern for her showing in the way he looked at her.

"I'm fine. Before I went to sleep last night, I thought about Jacob as the Town Marshal. What's going to happen when Becker comes back to town and finds Jacob has taken over his office? You did say Becker was not in town when you captured those men and put them in jail, didn't you?"

"Yes, I did. Jacob will have the backing of the town council and a deputy. If Becker gives him any trouble, I suspect Jacob will have to arrest him."

"Oh, I see," she replied thoughtfully. "But don't you think that will cause more trouble?"

"It might, but Jacob is a good man and he's smart. He won't push it unless Becker does. I doubt Becker has the nerve to challenge Jacob."

"I'm sure you're right," she replied.

"Becker knows Jacob is good with a gun and he is a capable man. Becker would be hard pressed to challenge Jacob without help."

At that moment there was a knock on the door. Sam turned around and opened the door. He saw Bill standing on the porch with his hat in his hands. The look on his face showed he was worried about something.

"What is it, Bill?"

"Well sir, you said you wanted to know if I remembered who was ridin' that horse I'd seen the other day. You know, the one I said I'd seen 'fore?"

"Yes, I remember."

"Well, I think I remember who I'd seen ridin' it."

"Who, Bill?" Sam asked impatiently.

"I'm not a hundred percent sure 'cause she was some distance away, but I think it was old man Gregory's granddaughter."

"You mean Marie?" Sam asked with surprise.

"Yeah, that's the one. The reason I think it sorta stuck in my mind was I ain't never seen her in pants 'fore. I'd only seen her in dresses and ridin' in that fancy buggy. I guess that might be the reason I wasn't real sure it was her 'til I had some time to think on it."

"You're telling me you saw Marie Gregory riding that horse?"

"Yes, sir. I seen her ride it up to the stable 'fore all them people arrived for the new barn raisin'. I got there sorta early, 'fore some of the others, you know. I don't think she knows I seen her. I was a bit far from her. But now I've had some time to think on it, I'm pretty sure it was her."

Sam had not gone to the barn raising at Carter's place because Frank Gregory would be there. Sam thought it would be best to stay away from Frank because he didn't want to cause any trouble, but three or four of his ranch hands had gone to help. What Bill said gave Sam something to think about.

First of all, he had never seen Marie in riding pants, although he was sure she probably had them. Secondly, he didn't get much of a look at who it was that had shot at them and then rode off in a hurry. It didn't seem likely to him it was Marie, but then it could have been anyone, including Marie.

The more Sam thought about it, the harder it became for him to think it wasn't Marie. When the ranch hands saw the horse and rider running away, they were too far away for them to see if it was a man or a woman on the horse. At that distance, it could have been either.

Sam got to thinking about how angry Marie had gotten in town when he suggested her grandfather might have been the sharpshooter. He realized it wouldn't be the first time he had met a woman who could shoot a gun and shoot it well. If her grandfather had been a sharpshooter during the war, he might have taught his granddaughter the skills needed for shooting long distances.

Although the thought of Marie being the one doing the shooting seemed a little far fetched, it was something he could not ignore. He would have to consider it as one of several possibilities.

The one thing that kept haunting his mind was he had never seen the horse before. He had to admit he didn't know every horse Gregory owned, but the horse was different. It would stand out like a sore thumb among the typical ranch horses in the valley. It looked like it might have been one of those horses from Kentucky that could run like the wind.

That thought reminded him that Marie's grandfather was from the south, and that he had fought for the Confederate Army. Most of those kinds of horses were bred in the south. Was it possible he had one?

"Sam? Are you okay?" Helen said disturbing his thoughts.

"Oh, Yeah. I was just thinking about what Bill told me."

"You think Marie is part of all the shooting?" she asked as if she couldn't believe it herself.

"I don't know," he said as he let out a sigh. "I certainly hope not, but you saw the kind of temper she has."

"Yes, I did," Helen agreed, but chose not to say anything more about it.

"I better check on Casey," Helen added.

"Yeah, sure," Sam said, too deep in thought to really pay much attention to what Helen had said.

Helen turned around and went down the hall to the bedroom where Casey was, leaving Sam with his thoughts. When she stepped into the bedroom, she noticed Casey lying there awake.

"How are we feeling today," Helen asked with a smile.

"Some better, I think," Casey replied weakly.

"That's good. Can I get you something to eat?"

"That would be nice. Say, is the boss 'round?"

"Yes. He's in the living room."

"Could you ask him to come in here? I need to talk to him for a bit."

"Sure," she replied, then turned and left the room.

Helen found Sam sitting at his desk going over some papers. She didn't want to disturb him, but she was sure he would want to talk to Casey as soon as he could.

"Excuse me, but Casey is awake and would like to talk to you."

"How's he doing?" Sam asked as he pushed his chair back from the desk and stood up.

"He looks like he's feeling better. He's hungry. That's always a good sign," she said with a smile.

Sam smiled back as he walked past her. He was impatient to see Casey. He wanted to find out what had happened out there.

Sam got to the bedroom door and slowly opened it. He didn't want to disturb Casey if he had gone back to sleep.

"Hi. How are you doing?" Sam asked when he saw Casey was still awake.

"I could be some better, boss, but I'll make it," Casey replied.

"Good. Do you remember what happened out there? "

"I sure do. I got jumped by six or seven guys while I was waitin' for the fellas to roundup Carter's cattle. They wrapped me in barbed wire and drug me some distance. I think one of their horses must have stepped on my leg and broke it."

"Well, we got 'um. There's only four of them left alive, and they will hang."

"Yah caught up with them?"

"We sure did. They led us right to town. The four left alive are in jail. One of them may not live to hang. He was shot pretty bad."

"You think that was a good idea to jail them there? Don't yah think Becker will let'm out?" Casey asked.

"I don't think so. He doesn't have any jurisdiction over them. Jacob is the new Town Marshal now."

"Yah don't say. He's a good man. He'll make a good Town Marshal."

"I think so. You better get some rest. And don't you worry about anything. I put Jack in charge until you are ready to return to work," Sam said as he turned and started out the door.

"Say, boss?"

"Yeah?" Sam replied as he stopped at the door and turned back around to see what Casey wanted.

"I don't know how to say this excep' to just come out and say it. I'm not even sure it happened 'cause I was hurtin' kinda bad at the time."

"What are you getting at, Casey?"

"While them fellas was wrappin' me in that barbed wire, I thought I could hear a woman givin' 'um orders. I can't swear to it, but I think I did."

"A woman?"

"Yeah, a woman," Casey said again.

"Do you know who it was?"

"No, not really," Casey admitted after giving it some thought. "I was hurtin' some at the time, but I'm darn sure it was a woman who kept tellin' 'um to make it tighter."

"I don't recall seeing any tracks that led anywhere but to town. When we caught up with them, there wasn't any woman with them."

"Maybe she didn't go to town," Casey suggested.

"Maybe, you're right. Maybe she didn't," Sam agreed.

Sam looked at Casey for a moment while he thought about what he had been told. He also thought about what he could do to find out if someone else had been there giving orders.

"I think I'm going to take a couple of the hands with me and have a good look around again. I might find something. You get some rest. I'll be back to talk later."

"Sure enough," Casey said, then closed his eyes.

Sam looked at Casey for a moment before he left the room and quietly closed the door behind him. As he slowly walked down the hall toward the living room, he thought about what Casey had told him. This was the second time this morning that a woman had been mentioned as someone who might be involved in what was happening in the valley. It was too much for Sam to simply ignore.

Sam tried to think of all the women who lived in the valley. Most of them were the wives or daughters of hard working ranchers. There were a few women in town, but they were the wives or daughters of shopkeepers, except for the schoolteacher. He found it difficult to see any of those women involved in all that was going on.

Sam returned to his desk and sat down. It was hard for him to believe Marie might be involved in actually starting a range war. The more he thought about her and her temper, the more he felt she might be capable of such a thing. He had to wonder if she really knew how deadly a range war could become. Maybe she didn't care, he thought.

Frank Gregory was a bitter man who had lost his place after the Confederacy lost the war. It had been rumored that he had once owned a large plantation in South Carolina. Marie would have been old enough to have enjoyed the southern life style of the granddaughter of a plantation owner before the war began. She had probably had everything she wanted whenever she wanted it. She no longer had that out there.

Living under the influence of her grandfather and remembering what it was like to be rich and to have servants to do everything was probably eating at her. She might be trying to get some of that way of life back. If that was true, it might explain why Marie was like she was. It also might explain why Frank was so bitter.

Just then, Sam heard Helen come into the room. He turned and looked at her.

"Helen, how would you like to go for a ride with me this afternoon?"

She looked at him, then smiled. "I would love to. Where are we going?"

"Out to check on some tracks near where Casey was hurt."

The smile quickly left her face. She wasn't sure if she wanted to go out there again right now, but Sam seemed to want her to go with him.

"Sure," she replied somewhat reluctantly. "Will we be taking any of the men?"

"Yes. I'll make the arrangements and we'll go right after our noon meal."

Helen nodded she understood and then went out into the kitchen to help Margaret. As she prepared a tray for Casey, she wondered why Sam wanted her to go with him. It seemed to her to be something the men would do. She thought about asking him, but decided she would learn in good time.

CHAPTER TWENTY-TWO

Sam walked out onto the front porch of the ranch house and leaned the Winchester rifles he was carrying up against the porch railing. He then leaned against one of the posts on the porch to wait for Helen. While he waited, he sat down on the porch railing and drew his gun from his holster. He checked it to make sure it was ready for use.

Sam heard the sounds of footsteps in the dirt and looked up. He saw two of his ranch hands walking toward the ranch house. They were leading several horses including his black stallion, Midnight, and Helen's Palomino, Sunshine. When they got to the ranch house, he slipped his gun back into his holster and picked up the rifles.

He stepped down off the porch. Sam slipped one of the rifles into the scabbard on his saddle, then walked around to Helen's horse and put the other rifle in the scabbard on her saddle. He turned around in time to see Helen at the door.

When Helen came out of the ranch house, Sam quickly noticed she was prepared for the ride. From her appearance, he could see she was well aware of the dangers that existed in Elkhorn Valley. She was wearing her brother's gun on her hip.

"Ready?" Sam asked her.

"Yes."

Sam took the reins to Helen's horse and held them while she put her foot in the stirrup. He watched her as she swung gracefully into the saddle. He took the reins to his own horse. He slipped his foot in the stirrup, swung himself into the saddle and then looked at Helen to see if she was ready.

From the look on her face, she was as ready as she was ever going to be. He glanced over at the ranch hands to make sure they were ready before he pulled back on the reins and turned his horse away from the ranch house.

As they started out of the ranch yard, Sam told his ranch hands where they were going and for them to lead on. He then slipped in behind them so he could ride next to Helen.

"I'm sorry that times are such you have to wear a gun. I hope you don't have to use it, but if you do it's nice to know you have it."

"Why are we going out to where Casey was injured?" Helen asked.

"I'm hoping to find a set of tracks that might very well tell me who's responsible for all the shootings."

"Do you think it could be Marie?" Helen asked as she looked into his eyes for some indication of how he felt about her question.

Helen wasn't even sure why she asked him about Marie. He had already made it clear he had no feelings for Marie. She wondered if she might be a little jealous of Marie for occupying Sam's mind so much.

"I would hope not, but I have to find out."

"Why?"

"Why? So I can put a stop to the killing before it turns into a range war," he said as he looked at her.

"Do you still care for her?" Helen asked, almost instantly wishing she had not asked.

"No," he replied with a much sharper tone in his voice than he had intended.

He reached out and gently put his hand on Helen's arm.

"I have no feelings for her. But I hope she is not the one who killed your brother and has been shooting at me."

"Casey told you something this morning, didn't he? What did he tell you?"

Sam thought for a minute before answering her. He wasn't sure how much he should tell her, but he also didn't want to keep anything from her. He decided it would be best if she knew everything.

"Casey said he thought there was a woman nearby when they wrapped him in the barbed wire. He said he could hear her telling them to make the barbed wire tighter."

"Is that why we're going out there? So you can see if there are any tracks that might support his claim there was a woman there?"

"Yes."

"And what will you do if you find them?"

"I'll do what I can to have her arrested and stand trial, if there's enough evidence," Sam replied, then turned and looked straight ahead.

At this point in time, there was nothing more to be said. Helen had watched Sam very carefully as he answered her questions. She knew he had had feelings for Marie at one time, but she was now convinced more than ever that it was over between them. She believed Sam when he said his only interest in Marie was to find out if she was involved in the shootings in some way. Helen was sure the thought that Marie was involved in the killing of her brother and shooting at him had to make it hard for Sam.

It was a fairly long ride out to where Casey had been injured. It would take them awhile to get there, although not near as long as it had taken them with the wagon in the dark. The time gave Helen a chance to think, which she needed to do.

Helen rode along in silence, but her mind was speaking to her loud and clear. She wondered if her feelings for Sam might be clouding her opinion of Marie.

That thought made her think even more about what kind of a woman Marie was. She had to wonder if Marie was the kind of woman who could shoot a man in the back like her brother had been shot.

There had been no mistaking Marie's play for Sam. She had fluttered her long dark brown eyelashes at him and talked to him in a child-like sweet voice she used to charm him and to show him how innocent she was. Helen was glad to note Sam had not fallen for it.

Yet, Helen had seen Marie's temper, the mean look in her eyes when she was angry, and how angry and spiteful Marie could be. Helen had also seen how well Marie used her looks and charm to hide it. The more she thought about Marie, the more she believed there was nothing innocent about the woman. She was cold and calculating, and she knew exactly what she was doing.

It didn't take Helen long to start to understand Marie. It also didn't take long for her to believe Marie might very well be capable of shooting someone in the back. She believed Marie might be responsible, or at least had a good deal to do with some of what had been going on in the valley. Maybe Sam was right, she thought. Maybe Marie was interested in only two things, Sam's ranch and herself.

The real problem, as Helen saw it, was how were they going to prove Marie's involvement? With what little she knew about Marie, it would be hard to find anyone in the valley who would believe she was capable of shooting at someone, let alone killing a man in cold blood.

Helen turned her thoughts to Sam and his ranch. She had no problem understanding why someone like Marie would want to get her hooks into him. He had the nicest and largest ranch in the area, and he was probably the richest rancher in the Elkhorn Valley. But that was due entirely to his hard work and his dedication to his ranch. He had not gotten where he was by grabbing things from others or lording over them. He had built his ranch with blood, sweat and tears, and that was what Helen liked about him.

What she loved about him was the way he held her in his strong arms and the way he kissed her. She loved the feel of his strong body pressing against her when he held her tightly, and the warmth of his lips against hers made her want him.

It was those times she wanted more than anything. If Sam had only a small ranch with little to his name, she would still want him to hold her. She would still love him.

Helen's thoughts were suddenly disturbed by the sounds of gunfire. She looked around and saw Sam and the ranch hands jumping off their horses and running for cover in a small gully. Without even thinking, she jumped off her horse and scrambled down into a shallow ravine. She drew her gun and made ready, but for what she didn't know.

Helen had suddenly found herself all alone. From where she had found cover, she could not see where Sam and the others were. Everything had happened so fast she had not thought to grab the rifle Sam had put in the scabbard on her saddle.

The shooting had stopped as quickly as it had begun. Now it was quiet. She listened in an effort to hear something, anything that would tell her what was going on, but she heard nothing. Her heart was in her throat as she thought about Sam. Questions began to race through her mind. Was he all right? Had he been shot? Was he dead?

Sam had the same problem. He could not see Helen. Since she had been a little way behind them, he was not sure if she was hurt or not. In fact, he was not really sure where she was.

"Helen, are you all right?" Sam called out.

The sound of Sam's voice was like a breath of fresh air to a drowning person. She let out a long sigh before she answered.

"Yes. Are you?"

"We're fine. Did you see who it was?"

"No," she replied wishing she had been paying more attention to what was going on around her instead of wasting time thinking about Marie.

Helen rose up a little and looked over the edge of the ravine. At first she didn't see anything except wide-open spaces, but then she saw something move. It was just a hint of movement, but movement just the same.

Helen held her gun tightly in her hand as she watched to see if it might move again. She waited and watched. All the time she waited and watched, she wanted to call out to Sam to tell him about the movement. Helen decided to keep quiet rather than to alert whoever might be there that she could see them moving around.

The waiting was almost more than Helen could stand. She grew impatient and wanted so much to say something to Sam and the others. When she was about to let them know that there was someone or something over by a cluster of small trees and bushes about one hundred and fifty to two hundred yards away, she saw a flash of light. It was the sun reflecting off of a piece of glass or something very shiny.

Helen took her gun in both hands and pointed it toward the cluster of trees and bushes. She cocked the hammer back on the gun and then slowly pulled back the trigger. The gun jumped in her hands as the hammer slammed down on a cartridge. The air was filled with the sound of her gun firing.

It was immediately followed by the sound of a rifle shot that came from the bushes. Helen didn't see where the shot came from and she was not sure where her shot went, but she had managed to rattle the nerves of whoever was shooting at them.

Suddenly, Helen saw a horse and rider disappear over a knoll behind the bushes. The rider had a rifle clutched in one hand and was leaning down over the horse's neck as the horse quickly disappeared over the knoll.

"There he goes," Helen shouted before she slipped back down in the ravine.

Helen took a minute to catch her breath. Although she had always been a good shot with a gun, she had never shot at anything so far away before, and certainly not at a human being. She suddenly found herself shaking uncontrollably and unable to move.

It was only a matter of seconds before Sam came running to her. He had heard the quiver in her voice and was worried about her. He slid down the side of the ravine and quickly moved to her side.

"Are you all right?" he asked, his concern for her showing in his face.

Sam took her in his arms and held her tightly. He could feel her body shake.

"I've never shot at anyone before," she said as she looked up at him.

"Well, we're glad you did. Whoever it was had us pretty well pinned down. You may not have hit him, but you sure scared him."

Sam gave Helen a chance to catch her breath while the others rounded up their horses. Once

Helen was ready, they mounted up and continued to move on toward where Casey had been attacked.

Helen found herself much more alert to what was around her. She tended to keep her eyes moving, looking for any little sign that would warn her of a pending attack. When they reached the place where Casey had been attacked, Sam and Helen got down off their horses while the ranch hands stood guard close by.

Sam started walking around in an ever larger semi-circle starting from a point close to where the break in the fence had been. He kept his head down as he examined the ground for anything he didn't think should be there. He found the tracks of the men who had wrapped Casey in barbed wire just as he had before. He was looking for anything he might have missed the first time.

When he was about thirty feet or so away from where the break in the fence had been, he found a bare spot on the ground and another set of tracks made by another horse, one that had not gone into town. The hoof prints were smaller, but the stance of the horse indicated the horse was not all that small. And from the looks of them, the horse had been standing in one spot for some time.

Sam also found a single boot print in the ground next to where the horse had been. It appeared to be rather small for a man's boot print. Whoever had been on the horse had gotten off for some reason.

The only other tracks were those of one of the men they had followed into town.

As Sam knelt down and studied the tracks, he read it like this. The person with small feet had ridden to this spot, then got off the horse. One of the men who had been involve with tying Casey up with the barbed wire had walked over to the person with small feet. They probably talked for a minute or so. The man then went back to do his dirty work. When the men rode off to town, the rider with the small feet mounted up and rode off in a different direction.

Since the tracks disappeared in the hard ground and dried grass, Sam was not sure where the lone rider had gone. The only thing he was sure of was the horse had not followed the others into town.

Sam was having a problem trying to figure out who the rider with the small feet was, and where he went. It looked as if the rider had gone along the fence, but the hard ground made it too hard to track.

Helen walked up beside Sam and knelt down beside him. She watched him as he studied the tracks and looked off along the fence.

"There was another rider here. From the looks of the tracks it could have been a woman," Sam said.

"You think it was Marie?" Helen asked.

"I don't know, but it could have been. From the looks of the tracks of her horse, it might have been that Kentucky horse Bill saw her riding."

"What do we do now?"

"I think it's time to confront her with what we know," Sam said thoughtfully.

"I doubt you have enough evidence to prove anything," Helen reminded him.

"I know, but we have to do something to stop all this shooting," Sam said with a note of frustration in his voice. "If she is involved, just the fact we know she is might be enough to get her to stop."

"Do you really think so?" Helen asked.

Sam looked at Helen before he answered, "No, not really. She has already gone too far. She would not quit now."

Just as Sam stood up and reached down to help Helen up, dirt flew up in front of him. It was quickly followed by the sound of a rifle firing. Sam pushed Helen aside as he dropped to the ground. He quickly turned and looked toward where the shot had come from. He saw that same horse and rider turn and start off across the prairie.

Sam sprang to his feet and ran to his horse. He jumped into the saddle, kicked the horse in the ribs with his spurs and started off across the prairie in pursuit of the shooter.

Helen got to her feet and ran for her horse. She knew she could not catch up with Sam's bigger and faster horse, but she had to follow him. The ranch hands quickly joined in and rode along side Helen as they raced across the prairie after Sam and the shooter.

Sam could see the horse and rider up ahead of him as he raced after them. He could still not tell who the rider was, but he was not about to let him out of his sight, if at all possible.

The horse he was chasing was fast and Sam quickly discovered his big stallion could not catch up with it. He also realized he was not getting left behind, either. The only hope he had of catching up was if his horse could outlast the Kentucky bred horse.

Sam lost sight of the horse and rider as they went over a knoll. When Sam reached the top of the hill, he saw the horse and rider disappear into a wide ravine with lots of cottonwood trees and undergrowth.

When the horse and rider failed to come out of the brush on the other side, Sam reined up and stopped quickly. He quickly realized for him to ride on down the hill and into the ravine would be next to committing suicide. The rider was far enough ahead of him that he would have time to take cover and get set up to pick him off as he came down the hill. Since Sam could no longer see the rider, and he was out in the open, he quickly wheeled his horse around and rode to the only available cover, the top of the hill.

Sam had reached the top of the hill when dirt kicked up near his horse's hoofs and the sound of rifle fire filled the air again. Sam didn't stop until he was well over the top and protected by the hill from the shooter.

CHAPTER TWENTY-THREE

Sam knew whoever was shooting at him would stand a good chance of getting away. But without cover for himself, he would not be able to get close enough to capture him.

He could see Helen and the others coming toward him. He reined up and waited for them. Helen was running her Palomino at a pretty good clip with his ranch hands right behind her.

Sam stepped out of the saddle and stood next to his horse while he waited for them to catch up to him. Helen reined up and looked down at Sam.

"What happened?"

"He got away. On the other side of the hill there's a ravine with a lot of cover. I decided it was not a good idea to go charging down there."

"That was probably a good idea," Helen agreed as she stepped down out of the saddle.

Sam started leading his horse back the way they had come. As he walked along, Helen walked along beside him.

Helen could tell by the look on Sam's face that he was disappointed, but she decided not to say anything about it. It was clear he was thinking about something and she didn't want to disturb his thoughts. She would patiently wait for him to tell her what was on his mind.

After walking for some distance, Sam stopped and looked at Helen. He didn't say anything for a moment or two. It was as if he was trying to make some sort of a decision, but wasn't sure about what he should do.

"We're going into town," he said suddenly.

"Why? What are we going there for?" she asked, confused by his decision.

"I've got a feeling our shooter will be heading straight for town."

"What makes you think that?" Helen asked, not understanding what compelled him to think that way.

"I don't know. It's just a hunch, I guess."

Helen looked at him for a minute as she thought about it and then smiled.

"Okay," she agreed, but wasn't sure why.

They mounted up and galloped off across country toward the road that would take them into Shallow Creek. In doing so, they had to cross part of Will Carter's land. They all kept their eyes open for any signs of his ranch hands, but they saw nothing but weak and starving cattle. The sight of the cattle simply confirmed what Sam already believed, Carter had given up. He was no longer making an effort to save the cattle or his ranch.

By the time they reached the edge of town, the sun was beginning to set behind the mountains. The four of them slowed their horses to a walk, then stopped outside of town to look around. Sam had been ambushed once already and didn't want it to happen again. He may not be as lucky the second time.

As they sat in their saddles looking around, Sam noticed there were several horses tied in front of the saloon. He recognized one of them as one of Will Carter's horses. That meant Will was probably in the saloon with some of his men, and he was getting meaner and meaner by the drink.

"Sam, look over there," Helen said as she reached out and touched his arm.

Sam turned and looked at what Helen was looking at. It was the same horse he had chased across the prairie just a little while ago. It was tied to the hitching rail down the street in front of the general store.

"Bill, is that the horse you saw Marie riding?"

"Yes, sir. It sure looks like it."

Sam looked over the town. He wasn't sure what he was looking for, but he didn't want any surprises. He was thinking about what he should do next. The one thing he had to know was who had been riding the horse in front of the general store. It would do no good to go down to the general store at this hour as it would be closed.

Sam glanced up at the sky. It would be dark soon. That could be to their advantage, or it could work against them. It took him a few minutes to decide what to do.

"Bill, take Helen and go around behind the saloon and wait for me to call for you. Jack, you go with them, but cover me from the back of the saloon."

"What are you going to do?" Helen asked.

"I'm going in the front door and see who's there."

"What if trouble starts?" Helen asked.

"Jack will cover me from the back of the saloon. I also have a friend in the saloon who will be on my side, Jake."

Helen didn't like what Sam was planning on doing, but she couldn't think of a better plan at the moment. She knew there was no way she would be able to talk Sam into letting it be. She also knew a full-blown range war would soon begin if something wasn't done to stop it. Reluctantly she went with Bill and Jack.

While Bill and Jack took Helen around behind the buildings to the back of the saloon, Sam sat on his horse and waited for them to get into position. While he waited, he took time to look around the town to see if any lanterns were being lit in any of the other buildings.

The one thing he immediately noticed was there were no lanterns burning in the jail. That struck Sam as a little strange. As far as he knew there were prisoners in the jail. He didn't think it would be like Jacob to leave them unguarded.

Sam looked back at the horses in front of the saloon. He studied them for a minute or two before he realized that at least two of them he had seen before. They had belonged to the men he and his ranch hands had jailed yesterday. Something had to have gone wrong if they were tied in front of the saloon.

Sam turned his horse, then slowly and quietly rode around behind the jail. He drew his gun as he rode up close to the back of the jailhouse next to a jail cell window.

Being as careful as possible he looked in, but he could not see anything as it was too dark inside the jail. He took a minute to think before he decided to speak.

"Jacob," he called out in almost a whisper.

"Sam, is that you?" Jacob whispered back.

"Yeah. What happened?"

"We were surprised by Becker and Will Carter. Becker shot Joe, then they let our prisoners out and locked us up."

"So Becker is in on this."

"Yeah, he sure is and I want him."

Sam could hear the anger in Jacob's voice, but he would have to wait to get his revenge on Becker.

"Are you all right?"

"I'm all right, but Joe's been hurt pretty bad. I've been doing the best I can for him, but it doesn't look good."

"Is there anyone else in there?"

"No. They all went over to the saloon."

"I'll let you out."

"The backdoor's locked from inside."

"I'll go around to the front," Sam said.

Sam stepped down out of the saddle and tied his horse to one of the bars on the window. He very carefully worked his way around to the front of the jail. He ducked inside, being very careful not to be seen.

Once inside the jail, he found the keys to the jail cells lying on the desk. He picked them up and unlocked the door to the cell where Joe and Jacob were being held.

"Joe's unconscious, but he's still alive," Jacob said.

"There's nothing you can do for him here. Go see if you can find Doc Miller and get him over here. He might be able to help Joe."

"What are you goin' to do?"

"I'm going across the street," Sam replied with a determined look on his face.

"Wait for me," Jacob said.

"How many are there?" Sam asked ignoring Jacob's request.

"The two we had in here, plus Becker and Will Carter as far as I know. The guy that was gut shot died. The one that was shot in the elbow is over at Doc Miller's. He's chained to a bed so he can't go nowhere."

"Okay. You go get Doc."

Jacob hesitated for a second before he did as he was told. He slipped out the front door of the jail and ran around the corner. He worked his way behind the buildings to where he could cross the street to Doc Miller's office without being seen.

Meanwhile, Sam stepped out of the jail. He looked across the street at the saloon. After taking a deep breath, he checked his gun and slipped it back in his holster. He then started across the street.

On his way across the street, he glanced down toward the general store. The horse he had chased earlier was still standing there. He had not gotten close enough to see who had been riding it when he was chasing it. However, the thought crossed his mind it could have been Marie.

Sam quickly turned back to the job at hand and chastised himself for letting his mind wonder. It was time to concentrate on what had to be done. It puzzled Sam as to why the horse had been tied up in front of the general store if the store was closed. Sam quickly came to the conclusion that the only way he was going to find out was to cross the street to the saloon and confront whoever was there.

As he approached the front of the saloon, he could see inside. Bart, the kid, Will Carter and Becker were all standing at the bar. Jake was pouring a beer for Will Carter. Jake didn't look too happy about serving them.

Sam noticed how tough they were talking. As Sam stepped up along side the door, he could hear Becker talking about how easy it had been for him to shoot Joe.

"That kid was sure slow with a gun," Becker laughed.

"Yeah," Bart chuckled. "He didn't even clear leather before you put a hole in him."

Sam stepped inside the bar, moved quickly to the side, planted his feet and prepared himself to draw his gun. He was ready for a fight. If anyone was stupid enough to move, there was a good chance he would die right where he stood.

"I suggest you turn around real slow. Any fast moves and you will find out how fast you can die," Sam said with the authority of someone who could back up what he said.

The four men at the bar froze right where they were for a couple of seconds. Slowly, they set their glasses down on the bar and began turning around, all except for Bart. He didn't turn around. He stood with his hand still on his glass as he looked in the mirror behind the bar.

With three of them now facing him, Sam kept a close eye on Bart. He knew if trouble were to come, it would come from him. Bart was not a smart man. He considered himself to be fast with a gun, stronger than most men, and able to take on anyone under any circumstances.

Bart had already been outsmarted by Sam before. He was not about to let it happen again. He would not go back to that two-bit cow town jail to wait for some judge to sentence him to hang.

Suddenly, Bart let go of his glass and started to swing around. As he did, he crouched down slightly while reaching for his gun. His gun had just cleared the top of his holster when a shot rang out filling the saloon with the smell of burnt gunpowder. The bullet from Sam's gun straightened Bart up and slammed him back against the bar with a hard jolt. Bart's knees buckled and the gun fell from his hand. Bart fell forward crashing to the floor. He was dead before he hit the floor.

The other three had seen the quickness with which Sam had drawn his gun, and the accuracy in which he placed a single bullet square in the center of Bart's chest. Wisely, they stood without making a move.

"You want to try me, Becker? It won't be so easy for you to put a hole in me," Sam said, hoping Becker would try.

Becker stood there looking at the business end of Sam's gun. It was easy for him to see he would not stand a chance against Sam, even in a fair fight.

"I didn't think so. Drop your gun belts on the floor," Sam ordered.

All three of them slowly and carefully reached for the buckles of their gun belts and loosened them. They all let their gun belts drop to the floor at their feet.

"You wouldn't be so brave if you didn't have that gun," Will said, his voice slurred by the liquor he'd been drinking.

"You wouldn't either if it wasn't for all the drinking you've been doing. I'm not going to take you on," Sam replied. "You're drunk."

"Drunk or sober I can kill you with my bare hands. I don't think you've got the nerve to shoot an unarmed man," he said as he took a step away from the bar.

The other two at the bar straightened up and looked as if they might like to help Will in a fist fight against Sam, that was if Will could get to Sam without getting shot first. Just as they started to take a step forward, they were distracted by the sound of a voice coming from the back of the saloon.

"I wouldn't deal myself in on this if I was you," Jack said as he stepped out of a dark corner near the backdoor of the saloon.

Everything seemed to stop. All eyes, except for Sam's, went to Jack. Jack was standing there with his gun drawn. He looked like he was ready to shoot anyone who might want to deal themselves in on the fight between Sam and Will.

Will turned back and looked at Sam. There was fire in his eyes and a mean look on his face. He took a couple of steps toward Sam, then stopped as he looked at Sam's face.

"I don't think you want to try anything stupid," Sam said, as he looked Will in the eyes.

Suddenly, Will lunged forward to attack Sam. Sam was ready and quickly sidestepped Will. As Will went rushing past, Sam swung his gun down hard on the back of Will's neck sending him crashing to the floor in a heap. Will laid sprawled out on the floor, unconscious.

Sam turned back to the two remaining at the bar and said, "There has been enough killing," Sam said.

"I wouldn't count on it being over," came the sound of a voice from behind him.

Sam immediately recognized Marie's voice. He hesitated to turn around and look at her. There was no question in his mind she had a gun on him.

"Drop the gun, Jack, that is unless you want me to shoot your boss," Marie said without a hint of fear in her voice.

Sam could hear the threat in her voice. There was no doubt in Sam's mind she would shoot him. Sam turned his head a little to look over his shoulder at Marie. As he did, he also turned a little sideways. He could see Marie was watching Jack. Sam slipped his gun back in his holster without Marie noticing it. She was watching Jack too closely, as were the others. Sam turned back toward Jack. He watched as Jack looked to him for instructions.

"You better do as she says," Sam said calmly.

Jack hesitated for just a second or two before he dropped his gun on the floor. He watched as Becker quickly ran over and pushed Jack back way from his gun. Becker picked up the gun and pointed it at Jack.

"Get over there by your boss," Becker insisted.

Jack moved close to Sam making it so Becker could not see Sam's gun. He kept an eye on Becker. They knew Becker did not have the backbone to do anything on his own. However, since he was not on his own at the moment, there was no telling what he might do. It was time to be very careful and to wait for an opportunity to take control of the situation.

Sam slowly turned around and saw Marie standing just inside the door of the saloon. She had a gun in her hand and had it pointed at him.

"I'm sorry, Sam. I guess this isn't your day," Marie said with a slight smile as she looked up at him. "You've had control of this valley's water supply for long enough. It's time someone else had control of it."

"I suppose you are the one who is going to control all the water in the valley?"

"As a matter of fact, yes," she replied with a grin.

"You think it's going to be that easy?"

"Oh, yes. You see, I'm going to dam up the river so no one will get water without paying me for it, and paying me dearly. I'm tired of living on some small dirty ranch. I want more," she said with a tone of hate in her voice.

"By more, you mean you want to live like you did before the war that took your grandfather's plantation?" Sam asked calmly.

"Yes, that's just what I want."

"Haven't you forgotten one minor little detail?"

"I don't think so, but what did you have in mind?"

"I own the land all the way to the mountains."

"That may be true now, but it won't be as soon as you are killed by Sheriff Becker when you try to escape from jail. Since you have no heirs to your property, it will go up for public sale. I'm the only one in the valley who can afford to buy it."

"I don't think it will be that easy," Sam said, his voice remaining calm.

"That's what you think," she said with a smile. "I knew you would come to town, that's why I got here first."

The smug look on Marie's face showed how confident she was in her plan. She was convinced she had complete control of the situation. Nothing could stand in her way now, or was there.

Suddenly, Marie's eyes got big and she stiffened up. She had a shocked look on her face as if she had suddenly realized she was going to die.

"Drop the gun," Helen said from behind Marie.

"Kill him," Marie yelled to Becker.

In the sudden confusion of the moment, Becker hesitated for only a split second, but it was long enough for Sam to swing around, draw his gun and pull the trigger. Everything seemed to happen at once.

The room filled with the sounds of guns going off. When the smoke cleared and everything had settled down, Becker was lying on the floor with the front of his shirt covered with blood. He had tried to out gun Sam, but he failed.

Marie was lying on the floor in pain and holding her arm. Just as she pulled the trigger to shoot Sam, Helen had shoved her into one of the tables causing her to go crashing to the floor and injuring her arm.

As she fell, her gun went off and the bullet struck Jack, grazing his hip and knocking him down.

Sam was standing with his gun pointed at the kid who had been so surprised by all the commotion that he had frozen in place.

It was over when Jacob came running into the saloon. Sam and Helen explained everything to him. As Jacob was about to march Marie, Will and the kid over to the jail to lock them up, he stopped at the door and turned toward Sam.

"Don't leave. As soon as I get these three locked up, I'll be back," Jacob said.

"We'll be right here," Sam assured him.

CHAPTER TWENTY-FOUR

A couple of Sam's ranch hands helped clear the bar of the two dead men, Bart and Becker, while Jacob marched Marie, Will and the kid across the street to the jail. Jack was taken to the jail where Doc Miller was looking after Joe to have his wound looked after.

Now that the bar was quiet, Sam sat down at one of the tables in the saloon to wait for Jacob to return. Helen joined him at the table, sitting very close to him.

"You all right?" Sam asked her as he reached out and took hold of her hand.

"Yes," she replied softly, only too happy that he was safe.

"Say you two, how about a drink?" Jake said, his voice showing he was trying to lighten things up a bit.

"That sounds good," Sam replied.

"I could use one, too," Helen said.

Jake poured the drinks from a bottle he kept under the bar. It was real Kentucky bourbon he saved for only very special occasions.

"This is my very best stuff," he said proudly as he carried the drinks to the table.

After passing the glasses around the table, Jake sat down across from Sam. He raised his glass and said, "Here's to life."

"To life," Sam said as he clinked his glass against Jake's and then against Helen's glass.

As Helen touched her glass to Sam's she said, "Here's to a long life."

"I'll go along with that," Jake said with a wide grin.

Sam couldn't miss the look in Helen's eyes. There was no doubt she was happy things had turned out the way they had.

As Sam was finishing his drink, Jacob came into the bar. The three sitting at the table turned and watched him as he walked across the room toward them.

"Get everyone put up for the night?" Sam asked.

"Sure did. That Marie can be a handful. She's yelling for her grandfather, but I don't think he will be able to get her out of this one," Jacob said.

"Not this time," Sam agreed.

"Oh, by the way, Sam, I thought you might like to know Marie was riding the Kentucky horse in front of the general store. When I went to get Doc Miller, I noticed there was a 40-60 caliber rifle in the scabbard."

"I had a feeling she might be one of them shooting at us. My guess would be her grandfather was the other," Sam said.

"You'd be right. Marie is screaming her grandfather will kill us all. She let it slip he was the one who killed Johnny."

Sam looked over at Helen. He could see she was saddened by the mention of her brother.

"Frank Gregory is bound to come into town to find Marie," Sam said.

"Yeah. And when he does, I'll arrest him. We can let the judge sort it all out from there," Jacob said with a smile.

"Good idea. It looks like you have everything under control."

"Yup," Jacob said with a slight grin.

"You planning on staying on as Town Marshal when this is over?" Jake asked.

"Yup, I think I will," Jacob said with a big grin. "Might even run for County Sheriff since they are in need of a new one."

"Good," Helen said. "You will be good for this town, and for the county."

"Thank you, Ma'am. I'll do my best."

"I'm sure you will," Sam said.

"You'll have to excuse me, but I've got to look after my prisoners," Jacob said as he stood up.

Jacob tipped his hat to Helen, then turned and walked out of the saloon.

As soon as Jacob had left, the saloon turned quiet. Everyone had left except Sam, Helen and Jake. Sam took a moment to look around the room.

Two men had died in this room on this very day, but there was a good possibility that an all out range war had been prevented. There was no doubt in Sam's mind that if a range war had broken out, there would have been a lot more dead bodies to bury.

"How about another drink," Jake suggested. He was beginning to think it was a little too quiet for a saloon.

Sam looked at Helen and then turned to look at Jake.

"As much as I would like to stay here and drink with you, I think we need to get back to the ranch. We have a lot to do. I hope you don't mind?" Sam said as he stood up.

"No, I understand. Stop in the next time you're in town. I'd be pleased to buy you another drink."

"We'll take you up on that," Helen said, then stood up.

Sam took Helen by the arm and led her out of the saloon. They stopped on the boardwalk out front when they saw Bill coming across the street toward them. He had a bit of a smile on his face and Sam wondered what was going on.

"Hi, boss."

"Hi, Bill. What's up?"

"I was talkin' to the Doc. He said that Joe will be laid up for awhile, but should recover okay. Jack should be up and around in a day or two. Both of them will be laid up for a spell."

"I'm glad they will be all right," Helen said.

"I was thinkin' if you don't mind, I'd stay in town for a couple of days to help Jacob keep an eye on things around here. At least until the judge gets here."

"I guess that would be all right. I'm sure he could use the help. We won't need guards around the place now, so we should be able to handle the workload without you for a few days."

"Thanks, boss. I'll see you in a couple of days."

"Sure thing," Sam replied.

"I guess that leaves you and me to go back to the ranch tonight," Helen said as she turned to look at Sam.

"I guess we best get started."

"I'll meet you here. My horse is out back," Helen reminded him as she pointed toward the back of the saloon.

"Okay. Midnight's out behind the jail."

Sam watched as Helen turned around and went back inside the saloon. As soon as he saw her disappear out the back, he went across the street and around behind the jail. He untied Midnight then swung up in the saddle. He arrived out in front at almost the same time as Helen.

Sam turned his horse toward home. Helen quickly moved up beside him. They rode at a pace that was both easy on the riders and the horses. It had been a hard day and they were caught up in their own thoughts as they rode toward the ranch.

When they turned onto the lane that would take them to the ranch house, Sam felt the first drops of rain. He stopped and looked up at the sky. He could not see a single star in the sky. For the first time in several months, it looked like they might actually get some rain.

"Did you feel that?" Sam asked.

"Yes," Helen replied with a smile on her face and bit of laughter in her voice.

The air began to fill with the fresh smell of rain as it began to rain harder. Sam smiled at Helen, then kicked his horse in the ribs and started for the barn. Helen followed close behind him.

Before they got to the barn the rain had turned into a steady downpour. By the time they got inside the barn, they were soaking wet. They pulled up and stepped down from their horses. Sam led his horse into a stall and took his saddle and bridle off. Helen led her horse into the stall next to Midnight's.

As soon as they had their horses wiped down and bedded down for the night, they walked back to the open door of the barn. They stood in the open doorway and watched the rain come down and turn the dry ground to mud. It was the prettiest sight they had seen for a long time.

Sam reached over and slipped his arm around Helen's narrow waist and gently pulled her up against his side. She smiled up at him as she slid her arm around behind him and leaned up against him.

They spent the next few minutes standing close to each other watching it rain. The smell of the rain and sound of it on the roof of the barn was soothing. It signaled new life to the ranch, to the prairie and to the entire valley.

"Stay here with me," Sam whispered softly.

"Yes," she replied as she turned in front of him.

Sam took his arm from behind her and took her by the hand. He led her back away from the barn doors. He took her in his arms and pulled her close to him.

Helen reached up and wrapped her arms around his neck. As she pressed her body against him, she tipped her head back and looked up at him.

Sam leaned down and kissed her. It was a passionate kiss meant to tell her that he wanted her to stay with him, not just for tonight, but for a lifetime.

Helen quickly melted into his arms as he slid his hands down her back. The feel of his hands on her and the feel of his strong chest pressing against her breasts wasn't enough. She wanted more of him.

"I want you," she whispered softly in his ear.

Sam looked down at her, then let go of her. He took her by the hand and led her to the ladder that went up into the hayloft.

"Wait here," he whispered. "I'll be right back."

Sam went back and closed the barn doors, then went into the tack room. He removed a bedroll and a blanket from one of the saddles.

When he returned to Helen, he pointed up the ladder then followed her up into the loft where he spread the bedroll out on the loose hay. Sam gently picked her up and laid her on the bedroll, then laid down beside her.

As he laid down, she reached up and pulled him down over her. She kissed him with all the love and passion she could find in her heart and body. It wasn't long before they had stripped each other of their wet clothes and were making love while outside the clouds had opened up and let the rain cover the ground giving it new life again.

After their passion had subsided a bit, Sam pulled the blanket over them and wrapped Helen in his arms. They quickly fell asleep to the sound of a gentle, yet steady rain.

When morning came and Helen opened her eyes, the first thing she saw was her clothes in a pile next to the blanket. Sam was curled up behind her back. She was wrapped safely in his strong arms. She could feel his strong body nestled against her back. His breath was gently blowing her hair on the back of her neck as he slept. She could not help but smile to herself as she put her hand over his and gently pressed it to her breast. She closed her eyes and let the feel of his hand caress her.

For the first time since she had come to Elkhorn Valley everything seemed right. She could hear the sound of the rain as it continued to fall, only now it was a gentle rain. It was the kind of rain that would soak into the ground and bring life back to the land. She knew she would spend the rest of her life there in Elkhorn Valley with the man she loved on the land he loved.

Printed in Great Britain
by Amazon